KILLER TRAIL

Center Point
Large Print

KILLER TRAIL

JOSEPH CHADWICK

CENTER POINT LARGE PRINT
THORNDIKE, MAINE

This Center Point Large Print edition
is published in the year 2025 by arrangement with
Golden West Inc.

The text of this Large Print edition is unabridged.
In other aspects, this book may vary
from the original edition.
Printed in the United States of America
on permanent paper sourced using
environmentally responsible foresting methods.
Set in 16-point Times New Roman type.

ISBN: 979-8-89164-457-1

The Library of Congress has cataloged this record
under Library of Congress Control Number: 2024948301

CHAPTER ONE

Will Shannon stalked the little Sonoran deer during most of the morning, and finally, seeing it browsing in a clump of spiky desert growth a hundred yards away, he caught it in his Winchester's sights and took up the trigger's slack. All the while he'd played hide and seek with the animal, he had figured that a batch of venison would save him the butchering of one of his Slash S steers, which would bring, come fall, maybe twelve dollars each on the Willcox market. And twelve dollars to a raggedy-pants cowman was . . . well, twelve dollars.

The buck stopped browsing, raised its antlered head, and looked about as though sensing danger. Shannon found himself gazing into a pair of limpid brown eyes and, that instant, feared he would go on having costly beef on his table. He doubted that he had the heart to take the buck's life.

Hell, this is loco, he told himself. *Steer or deer, it makes no difference which an hombre kills.*

His own eyes—a smoky gray in color and deep-set in his leathery, angular face—wavered briefly, then returned resolutely to the rifle's sights. He had laid aside his hat, and a vagrant breeze stirred his thick mane of faded yellow hair. The same breeze must have carried his scent to the deer, for the animal now knew there was danger and went bounding off, out of harm's way.

Having lost his chance to stock his larder with venison, Shannon swore under his breath at being so soft hearted. Then through the desert's stillness he heard a distant popping sound that he knew from experience could only be gunfire.

His first alarmed thought was *Apaches!*

His second was that his ranch buildings were being raided.

He grabbed his hat, rose from his prone position, and started running toward the arroyo where he had left his horse. A tall man, wide shouldered and lean hipped, he ran awkwardly on his high-heeled boots and rider's legs. But he covered distance almost as swiftly as the frightened deer, frantic with fear for the people at the ranch. He plunged through dense brush, and the barbs of cholla, ocotillo, and prickly pear tore at his clothing and flesh.

He dropped into the arroyo and caught up the horse's trailing reins. A zebra-striped dun, the animal was spooked by his headlong approach and shied away when he sought the left stirrup. He swore at it with angry impatience and rapped it across the nose with the barrel of his rifle. Then he was mounted and with a wild yell and a jab of spurs forcing the horse to carry him out of the wash.

His sister Kate and her husband, Phil Amhurst, were at his place, out from Valido, thirty miles away, to visit with him for a few days. Pete Amado, his hired hand, was with them, but Pete would be as nothing against a swarm of *bronco* Apaches, who were maybe drunk on the crude beer called *tiswin* that they brewed from fermented corn mash. His one hope was that the three had had time to barricade themselves in the little adobe house, which he had built with a stout door and loop-holed window shutters against the possibility of an Apache attack.

Shannon ran the dun as he'd never before run a horse in his thirty-two years. He ran it recklessly across the broken, brush-grown land. He peered ahead but was not yet close enough to see his squat buildings. No smoke, though. That was encouraging. The Apaches usually applied the torch to climax a successful raid. But maybe . . . maybe they weren't yet done with their victims. Expert at torture, they liked to see white-eyes die slowly—very, very slowly.

Shannon told himself that the shots hadn't necessarily been fired at his place. The shooting could have been off in another direction. And others than Apaches might have done it. The latest report, which he'd had from his brother-in-law, was that General Crook had chased Geronimo into Mexico and that the equally bloodthirsty Delgado was playing the role of reservation blanket Indian. But Geronimo could have sneaked back across the border and Delgado could have slipped away with a bunch of disgruntled bucks any dark night.

There, the buildings!

The grubby little house, the barn with the attached corral.

Shannon reined the dun to a walk and stood in the stirrups for a better look. No sound of shooting now, and no half-naked warriors rampaging about the buildings. But three men stood in the yard. White men, so far as he could tell. He felt no sense of relief, for when white men turned renegade they could out-Apache even Geronimo and Delgado. Shannon knotted the dun's reins and let go of them, wanting both hands free for his rifle.

Two of the men got onto their horses. The third remained standing beside his mount. This one seemed to be waiting for Shannon, whom he had seen, as though he had business to discuss with him. He held his rifle in his right hand, its stock resting against his hip.

Shannon saw none of his people. He saw nothing to tell him that anything was amiss. But he felt that something was very wrong. Coming within easy rifle range, he reined in the dun and stared at the man with the ready weapon. A giant of a man. And a black man at that.

"You there, hombre! Walk out here . . . alone!"

"Yas, sah, boss," the Negro called back, his mocking tone belying the servility of his words. "Ah come out there quick as ah can."

He moved forward half a dozen steps, then whipped his rifle up and drove a shot at Shannon. The report was the thunderclap of a Sharps buffalo gun. The slug caught the dun in the head, and though the animal was certainly dying that instant it bounded forward as though attempting to buck. Then it collapsed. Shannon threw himself clear to avoid being pinned beneath its body. He landed on his feet but lost his balance and went sprawling. He fell on a sharp rock, and pain stabbed his left side. He lay stunned for a moment, then he shoved himself to his knees.

The black man grinned wolfishly, a gold tooth glinting among the mouthful that gleamed whitely against the jet black of his skin. A jagged scar ran across his left cheek, from the corner of his mouth to the lobe of his ear. He stood inches taller than Shannon's six feet of height, and he was half again as thick through the body as the rancher.

"You listen to me, boss man." His voice had lost its mock servility; it was harsh, arrogant. As he spoke he shoved a fresh .50 caliber cartridge into the breech of his Sharps. "I could have put that slug into you as easy as into your horse, ofay. You lift that rifle you're holding, I'll do for you. Another thing . . . you come after me, I'll make buzzard bait of you. You heed my words, mister!"

He backed off to his horse, took hold of its reins, and led it across the yard as he continued to move backward. The two others had already ridden out. Now he swung onto his mount, which was as black as he, and rode after them. He went at a lope.

Shannon reared up and fired after him as fast as he could work his Winchester's trigger and hammer. His every shot missed. At the moment, badly shaken and raging as well, he couldn't have hit the side of a barn at point-blank range. Still, he kept shooting until the three became lost to his sight in the brush.

Now getting hold of himself, Shannon strode to the ranch yard and found his worst fears realized. Murder had been done here. Phil Amhurst lay face down in front of the house, the ground about him stained red with his blood. Old Pete Amado was sprawled on his back over by the barn.

Kate, Shannon thought wildly. *My God, not Kate too!*

He ran toward the house, calling her name. The door stood open, and he saw her lying just inside. The front of her green gingham dress was all blood. Her eyes were open and staring . . . staring lifelessly. A shotgun lay beside her: his shotgun. He knew then how death had come to her. She had heard the shooting outside and had armed herself. One of the trio had shot her when she appeared at the doorway, probably before she could fire the shotgun.

His mind reeling with the horror of it, Shannon turned from the doorway. He saw that his brother-in-law had tried to make a fight of it. Phil had come outside with the short-barreled .38 caliber revolver he had always carried when traveling. Shannon picked up and examined the gun. Phil had gotten off two shots, for all the good it had done him.

Shannon turned his brother-in-law onto his back to make sure life was really gone from him. He found no heartbeat. Phil's eyes too stared lifelessly. He had been a darkly handsome man of about forty-five and pretty much a dude in his way of dressing. A city-bred man, he had come from St. Louis a year ago in the hope of finding relief from a lung ailment in the dry desert climate. He'd bought out one of Valido's two general stores and done well with it.

Kate had been the teacher of the town's one-room schoolhouse with its dozen or so pupils, adding to her skimpy salary by doing dress-making on the side. Being nearly thirty years old, she had been, Shannon knew, resigned to spinsterhood until her first meeting with Phil. Love and marriage had come to that rather plain but extremely pleasant young woman, and Phil as well as she had seemed happy. They had excitedly broken the news to Shannon when they arrived at his ranch: Kate was expecting.

Shannon now swore bitterly, wracked by grief and the beginning of a terrible rage. He had loved Kate, and he had liked his brother-in-law. And they had been fond of him. They had come to visit him because Phil had wanted to make him a business proposition. He had offered to put up the money for Shannon to go on a cattle-buying trip down in Sonora. His idea had been for them to acquire a thousand head of stock cattle in a partnership deal.

"You'll never get anywhere with the few hundred head you own, Will," Phil had said. "You'll just go on living from hand to mouth forever. And go on being a hermit too. You should be working toward the future . . . thinking of the day when you'll marry and have a family."

Contented in his own marriage, Phil had wanted Shannon to find the same fulfillment. Shannon had liked the prospect of going partners with him, for he'd known that Phil had the touch, the ability to make any business pay. And now Phil Amhurst lay dead in the dust, already growing cold in the hot, brassy sunlight.

Why? What is the reason for it?

A groan from Pete Amado took Shannon across the yard to kneel beside the Mexican. Pete was bleeding from a wound at his left temple. He was gasping for air, his mouth hanging open and revealing broken, age-yellowed teeth. His lined, pockmarked face was gray with pallor. He uttered another agonized groan and tried to sit up. Shannon helped him, and supported him with an arm about his scrawny shoulders. Pulling off the old-timer's bandana neck scarf, he wiped away the blood. The wound was a nasty gash, but the flow of blood was slowing.

"What was it all about, Pete? Who were those bastards?"

The old vaquero gazed at him uncertainly. "Will? That you, Will?" His voice was a hoarse whisper.

Shannon picked him up and carried him into the barn, where the two of them had been bunking during the Amhursts' visit. He laid Pete on his blankets, then fetched a pail of water from the little creek that flowed past the buildings. He gave the semiconscious man a drink and washed his face clean of what blood remained. The wound needed bandaging, and Shannon went to the house, past Phil's body and, inside, that of his sister.

He got blankets from the bunks and covered first Kate and then her husband, thinking bleakly that they had been all the kin left to him . . . that now he was alone. Leaving Phil's shrouded body, he returned to the house for some cotton sacking and the bottle of whiskey he kept on hand for medicinal purposes.

In the barn again he gave Pete a drink of the whiskey and then used more of it to cleanse the man's wound. He ripped the sacking apart and bandaged Pete's head all around. After another drink from the bottle the Mexican was able to talk.

"That buggy horse of *Señor* Amhurst, Will . . . I just finished replacing the shoe it lost on the way out here. That's when those *hombres* rode in. They were in the yard before I saw or heard them."

His voice was still weak and shaky. The pallor hadn't left his face, which seemed, with its lines and wrinkles, its pockmarks and numerous small scars, a historical record of a seventy-year-long struggle for survival in this harsh and hostile land.

He had been turning the horse back into the corral when he saw the three riders come into the yard. He hadn't been wearing his gun, and one of them—a youth—had thrown down on him. One of the others was a half-breed, he said. And one a black man.

"*Mucho hombre*, Will. A big man, and strong like a bull."

"I saw him," Shannon said. "I saw him and, by damn, I won't forget him. What happened then?"

"The black man called for *Señor* Amhurst."

"By name?"

"*Si. Señor* Amhurst came to the door, then went

back inside. When he showed himself again, he had his gun. He asked what they wanted. The black man said, 'Boss, I want you. I've been wanting you, hunting you, for more than a dozen years.' The *señor* asked why he wanted him."

Pete pushed himself to a sitting position on the blankets. His voice was stronger when he spoke again.

"The black man said, 'Matamoros . . . you remember the ship at Matamoros, and the house?' Then he told *Señor* Amhurst to use his gun if he wanted. *Señor* Amhurst looked scared, but he lifted his gun and began shooting. He didn't hit anything. The black man laughed and shot him."

"And my sister, Pete?"

Pete choked up, tears welling in his eyes. He had known Kate a long time and had been fond of her. Finally he got it out. Kate had appeared at the doorway with the shotgun, and the youth—a wild kid, Pete called him—had shot her. The black man had yelled at him not to shoot, but too late. Pete had rushed at the youth in a rage and wanting to kill him with his bare hands. The youth had lashed out at him with his gun. That had been the last Pete had known until he regained his senses and saw Shannon there.

"She is dead, Will? *La señora*?"

Shannon nodded, his face grim and rock hard. "She's dead, Pete . . . and Phil too. You're lucky to be alive. So am I. That black man is a dead shot." He was silent for a moment, then went on, as though thinking aloud, "A strange thing . . . he could have done for me with no trouble at all. Why didn't he?"

Pete's anguished eyes searched his face. "You're not letting them get away with it, are you, Will?"

"No, I'm not letting them get away with it," Shannon said, his voice abrasive with rage. "It might have taken that black man more than a dozen years to find Phil Amhurst, but, damn his soul to hell, it won't take me that long to catch up with him!"

CHAPTER TWO

Without discussing the matter they decided what must be done. Pete would take the bodies to Valido, and Shannon would go after the killers.

Shannon hitched up a team and laid the blanket-wrapped bodies in his light spring wagon. With a boost from him, Pete got to the seat and took up the reins. With his head swathed in bandages and his face a sickly gray, he looked far from his normal self. Shannon eyed him dubiously.

"Valido is a long haul, *amigo.* You sure you can make it?"

"I'll make it," Pete told him. "You go after those killers. But take care, Will. All three are bad *hombres*, but watch out for the big one with the black skin. He is the worst—a man who laughs when he kills. You want me to tell the sheriff?"

"Yes, tell him," Shannon said. "Tell him I'll be tracking them, and that they headed west from here. If I don't catch up with them before dark, I'll come to town, then set out after them again after the funeral service."

He stepped back and watched the Mexican drive from the yard and take the north-running trace of a road. He worried for a moment, fearing that Pete might be in worse shape than he had let on and not hold out. With a shrug and a shake of his head he went to where his dead horse lay.

He found that he could grieve for an animal as well as for humans. He'd had the dun for nearly five years, having caught it running wild and unbranded in Comanche country. Although certainly once Indian owned, it had taken to white men's ways. He'd lost it to a thief in New Mexico but had found it wandering loose again. Because of its turning up this second time, he had named it Bad Penny. In a way he had made a pet of the dun, riding it far more than any of the half dozen other horses he owned. He would miss Bad Penny, all right.

He removed the bridle from the lifeless head, the bit from the slack mouth. He began working at the saddle, which was the better of the two he owned. A double-cinched rig, it was the handiwork of Joe Baca over in Navasota, Texas. Nothing fancy, but made almost to outlast a man's rump . . . and it fit his own as comfortably as a pair of old pants.

Finally getting the saddle off the dead horse, he carried the saddle, the bridle, and the saddle blanket to the corral. He went into the pen with his rope and dropped its loop about the neck of his next best bronc, a stocky blue roan. He saddled it and drove the other horses out of the corral to shift for themselves. He had no idea when he would be returning here.

If ever, he thought, with that big black man in mind.

He led the roan over to the house and left it ground hitched. Going inside, he packed his shaving gear, a clean shirt, a change of socks, and a few other articles into his war bag. He made a roll of a pair of blankets. He took a canteen down from a wall peg. That was it. He took a last look about the one-room house, again shrugged his shoulders, and shook his head. He wasn't leaving much behind, if he didn't make it back. He went out with his gear, pulling the door shut. After tying the war bag and blanket roll behind the cantle of the Navasota saddle, he went to the creek and filled the canteen. Hanging the canteen from the saddle horn, he mounted the roan and struck out in the direction the murderers had taken.

Their horses had left tracks in the dry, gritty soil almost plain enough for a blind man to follow, and Shannon was able to do his stalking of the three while he held his roan to a lope.

They were traveling fast, as though they expected him to come after them despite the black man's warning. By midafternoon Shannon knew he wouldn't catch up with them that day. Stopping to rest his horse, he debated whether to call off his manhunt temporarily. He decided against this, taking into account the fact that his quarry had changed direction at this point. They had swung due south, toward the Frio Hills.

The Frios were craggy uplifts thrusting starkly up out of the desert far from any beaten track. For some years a mad German named Brugher had worked a diggings at that lonely place until the Apaches had done for him. He'd had a well, Shannon recalled. The murderers might have known about the place and have set up camp there. Could be that they intended to spend the night in the hills.

After giving the roan a full hour of rest, Shannon struck out for the Frios. The hoof tracks he followed continued in that direction, die-straight. The sun was half down behind the west mountains when he entered the maze of bare slopes and sheer cliffs. Wary of an ambush, he dismounted with his rifle and led the roan. Minutes later he reached the gorge in which Brugher had tunneled into a cliff in search of a silver lode he'd never found.

Brugher's adobe hut was in ruins, its roof caved in and its walls crumbling. The tailings from his *inútil*—worthless—mine lay like a great landslide downward from its entrance. His well was located to one side of the hut, its circular stone wall rising three feet above the ground. It was shaded by a paloverde tree. Seeing a movement behind the tree's lacy yellow green foliage, Shannon let go of his horse and ducked behind a cluster of boulders. Peering from this cover, he saw a saddled horse there. It seemed tied to the tree. He remained where he was, looking carefully all about the high-walled gorge. He saw no other living thing, but uneasiness gripped him. He felt that the owner of that horse might be watching over the sights of a rifle, waiting for him to expose himself again and move within range of his weapon.

The sun was gone from the gorge, but Shannon began to sweat more profusely than he had during all the hours he had followed the murderers' tracks with the sun's hot glare bearing down on him. He was out of practice; he no longer had the iron nerve this sort of game required.

Once he'd been good at it. Back during the War he had served with Hood's Texas Brigade at a most unripe age. Later, after a spell of cow-boying, he had done a hitch with the Frontier Battalion—the Texas Rangers—and seen action first against the Comanches and then against outlaws, Anglo and Mexican. He'd served as a deputy sheriff, and he'd worked as a special agent for Wells Fargo. He had, in fact, played the grim game of manhunting for a considerable part of his life. But he had been ranching for three years now, and in that length of time any man became rusty at the trade he had given up.

Aware of this, Shannon soon became edgy. His patience running out, he shouted, "All right, you! If you're aiming to bushwhack me, make your try!"

He heard an answering call, seemingly from a great distance. He failed to make out the words, and he did not recognize the voice as that of the black man. Puzzled, he waited silently. His hands were clammily wet. He wiped them on his pants legs, then he took up his rifle again.

The voice called out again, and this time he caught the words: “Help me! Get me out of here, for God’s sake!” It was the voice of a panic-stricken man.

Shannon looked all about again, this time studying the mine entrance midway up the steep slope. He saw nothing up there, or anywhere. Dusk was thickening in the gorge.

Again came the panicky outcry: “Help me, help me!” And then, with anger, “Damn it, help me!”

Shannon realized that the voice was not distant but was somehow muffled. He rose and ventured from the rocks, moving warily toward the ruins of the hut. Then the cry for help came once more, and he located its source. He went to the well and looked into it, seeing dimly, ten feet below, a man standing in knee-deep water. It was one of the murderers: the young one, the one who had killed Kate. Shannon felt a savage sort of joy, a wicked satisfaction.

With help at hand, the youth got over his panic. “Get me out of here, you! Don’t just stand there gawking at me!”

Shannon said, “Why the hell should I get you

out?" Then, curiosity getting the better of him, he asked, "How'd you get down there, kid?"

"That black bastard threw me down. When I catch up with him, I'll—"

"Why'd he throw you down?"

"So you'd catch me."

"So I'd . . . now why would he do that?"

"He figured you'd come after us," the youth said, his tone now a plaintive whine. "He wanted you to kill me . . . or to turn me over to the law for hanging."

"I don't savvy any of this," Shannon said. "But getting you out of there . . . that will take some deciding. You're a woman-killing scum, and I'm not sure if I'll shoot you or take you in to be hanged. Maybe I'll leave you down there . . . so you're a long time dying and have plenty of time to think on what you did back at my ranch. I'll have a smoke while I make up my mind how it's to be."

He moved away from the well and got out makings for a cigarette. The trapped youth pleaded with him. He was a beggar now, tough no longer. Shannon remained unmoved. He was able to ignore that one. As he smoked his cigarette, he thought of the black man.

He knew I'd come after them and in leaving the kid behind he was throwing me a sop. He hoped I'd be satisfied with the one who murdered a woman.

Shannon's lips curled in a malicious grin.

"You're wrong, black man, dead wrong. I won't be satisfied until I've settled with all three of you bastards."

Returning to the well, he called down, "What's your name, kid?"

"Red Tyson. Get me out of here!"

"And the black man's?"

"Ben Murdock."

"The half-breed's?"

"Sanchez . . . just Sanchez."

"Why were the three of you after Phil Amhurst?"

"I don't know."

"You'd better know, if you don't want me to ride out and leave you to rot down there."

"You can't do it!" the youth wailed. "That ain't human!"

"Why did you want Amhurst dead?"

"I don't know. I swear it!"

"Red, I'll be riding. So long."

"No, wait! Listen, mister—please!"

"Shannon's my name, if you don't know it. Will Shannon."

"I don't know what it was all about, Mr. Shannon," Tyson said, sounding like a small boy on the verge of tears. "Murdock hired the breed and me to ride with him. A dollar a day and found. We were just hired hands. There was this tinhorn he wanted to kill, he said, and we were to throw down on anybody who tried to stop him."

"So the woman back there tried to interfere and you killed her."

"She had a shotgun!"

Trying to contain his rage, which threatened to get the better of him, Shannon said, "Murdock never told you why he wanted Amhurst dead?"

"No, he never. When I asked him once, he told me it was none of my business."

"Where was it he hired you and Sanchez?"

"Yuma."

"He hails from there, does he?"

"He's got a diggings up the Colorado from there," Tyson said. "He pans for gold. So he claims." Then, hysteria in his voice, he yelled, "Get me out, Shannon! It's getting dark and I'm scared!"

Still untouched by pity, Shannon ignored that. "How did he know Amhurst was at my ranch?"

"We went to Amhurst's store in Valido, and the clerk there told us."

"How old are you, Red?"

"Old enough, damn it."

"Yeah . . . old enough to shoot down a woman."

"Seventeen. I've been passing for a lot older, but that's all I am. Only seventeen."

"You know you'll hang, don't you?"

"I'd sooner hang than die down here!"

"All right," Shannon said. "I'll give you your choice."

He took a final drag on his cigarette, then went after his horse. He booted his rifle, swung to the saddle, and removed his catch-rope from the horn while riding to the well. He flipped the loop end of the lariat down to the youth.

"Sing out when you're ready, kid."

Hearing a yell from below, he kneed the roan into motion and hauled the youth up from the well. Scrambling over the wall, Tyson threw the rope aside and removed his boots to empty them of water. He was a runty kid, bonily thin. His homely face was a mass of freckles, and his rust-red hair stuck out raggedly from under his battered old hat. His boots were run down, his wet pants threadbare, his shirt the worse for wear. Not knowing him for what he was, Shannon would have felt sorrow for him. As it was, he had to fight against a rage-induced urge to pump him full of slugs. He might have ended it then and there by telling the youth to draw on him, but Tyson's holster held no gun. The black man had disarmed him before dumping him down the well.

Looking up, Tyson said, "Well, let's get going. Ain't no use hanging around here."

"That's right," Shannon said. "You'll do your hanging from a gallows."

"That gallows ain't built yet, mister."

"You're mighty cocky all of a sudden."

"I figure the law won't hang a kid. Send me to

prison, maybe, but not hang me. I'll claim I'm only sixteen . . . even fifteen."

Now Shannon couldn't hold his rage in check. "Kid, I promise you this: if the law doesn't hang you, I damn sure will. Now head for your horse."

He rode behind the youth to the paloverde tree where his horse, a surprisingly fine-looking sorrel, was tethered. He saw that the boot on its saddle held no rifle. The black man again. He'd really wanted the kid taken.

As Red Tyson untied and mounted the sorrel, Shannon got down from his roan and removed the coiled rope from the horn of the youth's saddle.

"What's the idea?" Tyson demanded.

Shaking out the lariat's loop, Shannon said, "I'm not giving you a chance to make a run for it in the dark. Let loose of the reins and raise your hands."

Tyson stared at him sullenly for a moment, then he kicked the sorrel into motion and reined it toward him. Shannon jumped aside in time to avoid being run down. The youth now swung his mount in the opposite direction, in an attempt to escape. Shannon made a throw with the rope, dropping the loop about him. Bracing himself, Shannon took the jolt as the lariat jerked taut. He hauled Tyson out of the saddle. The sorrel kept on running, and the youth hit the ground hard and lay stunned for a moment.

Then he burst out, "My back's busted! I can't move!"

"You'll move," Shannon told him, "or I'll drag you over to the well and throw you back down it."

Cursing bitterly, Tyson got to his feet. The lariat's loop was around his middle, and Shannon, moving up behind him, knotted the rope at the hondo so it couldn't be removed except with difficulty. After he played out the lariat, he got onto his horse and tied the end to his saddle horn.

"Now catch up your bronc," he said, "or it's back to the well with you."

Sullen of expression, Tyson started walking toward the sorrel. It had come to a stop a hundred yards down the gorge.

When his prisoner was mounted, Shannon told him, "One more stunt like that, I'll shoot you . . . with pleasure. I don't have to take you in for the law, remember. Stay abreast of me, to my left. Now move!"

They rode away from the abandoned diggings, leaving the gorge behind. Minutes later, as they came from the hills, a rock bounded down the last slope with a great clatter. It passed a short distance ahead of them. Doubting that the rock had started falling of its own accord, Shannon dropped from the saddle with his rifle. He crouched behind a boulder and stared up at the steep slope. All was darkness up there. He could make out nothing but a scattering of rocks, some of them large enough to conceal a man . . . even a man as big as Ben Murdock.

To Red Tyson, he said, "You move a muscle, kid, you're a goner." Then, lifting his voice in a shout, he called out, "All right, black man. . . . Play out your hand!"

Laughter from a rich bass voice floated down the slope, seemingly from the crest of it. Shannon could see nothing of the man. He didn't need to see Ben Murdock. He had the picture of him etched in his memory for all time: the breadth of him, the towering height; the gleaming white teeth with the gold one in the front, bared in a wolfish grin; the jagged scar across the left cheek of the ebon face. Shannon swore under his breath, hatred for the Negro roiling in him.

Murdock called out, that devil's laughter still in his voice, "Boss, I've got cat's eyes. I can see good in the dark, and I can see you . . . plain as day. That rock ain't hiding you none. I've got the sights of my old buffalo gun lined on you right now. I could pick you off easy."

Shannon's flesh crawled. He believed the man. He tried to make himself smaller behind the boulder.

"Listen, boss. . . ." Murdock spoke without laughter now. "I'm giving you your life. I ain't after killing you. I ain't got reason to want you dead. Not if you get off my trail. Now take that no-good kid in and see him hanged. He's the one who killed the woman. Ain't that enough to satisfy you?"

"Not by far, damn you!"

"Maybe you don't believe I could nail you, eh? Well, you just put your hat on that rock and I'll show you."

Shannon found the offer to his liking. He removed his hat from his head, placed it on top of the boulder, and lay prone at the side of the rock with his rifle aimed at the slope.

Murdock's shot came, the report of the buffalo gun again a thunderclap. Shannon's hat went flying. Marking Murdock's position by the muzzle flash of his weapon, Shannon pumped three fast shots at it. The sharp reports of the Winchester were still ringing in his ears when Murdock's mocking laughter came again.

"You ain't nowhere close, boss," the black man taunted. "You missed me by a mile." Then, his voice turning harsh, he added, "Now you listen and listen good. I ain't killing you now, because I don't like killing. I never did kill a man except he did me harm. You owe me something for letting you live, the way I figure. You can pay it by not coming after me and forcing me to kill you. You turn that fool kid over to the law and call it quits!"

"You listen, Murdock," Shannon yelled. "He wouldn't have killed my sister but for you!"

For a moment there was no reply, then the black man said, “You heed what I said, boss. So long.”

Shannon stared upward, straining to catch a glimpse of the big man in the hope of getting a clean shot at him. He saw nothing at all, and after a moment he knew that Murdock had gone.

Red Tyson had been silent all this while, but now he burst out, “Shoot him, Ben! Shoot the jasper and let me get away!”

Rising, Shannon said, “Save your breath, kid. He’s gone. And he wouldn’t have done what you want, anyway. He’s thrown you to the wolves, even though he knows it won’t keep me from coming after him. He has a loco way of thinking, that hombre.”

He looked for his hat. Picking it up, he found that it had two holes through the crown. Cat’s eyes. The black man could see in the dark, and he was a dead shot to boot. Taking him wouldn’t be easy, Shannon realized. It might be impossible. Trying to take him might get a man killed.

But I’ll be coming after you, black man!

Shannon walked to his horse, mounted it, and started away with his prisoner.

Red Tyson was uttering whimpering sounds now. He was bawling like the kid he was and had tried not to be. Shannon knew that it took all kinds of men to make the world, but these two, Red Tyson and Ben Murdock, sure took the prize for being odd ones. Now, as he rode through the darkness with the frightened kid, he wondered what sort of wrong Phil Amhurst had done Ben Murdock more than a dozen years ago. He couldn't imagine his brother-in-law, seemingly the most decent of men, having been capable of doing anyone harm. Still, who knew what any other man was really like? Weren't all men really strangers?

CHAPTER THREE

Riding into Valido with his prisoner at mid-morning, Shannon went directly to the courthouse. He had removed the restraining rope from Red Tyson at sunup, knowing the kid wouldn't be so foolhardy as to make a break by daylight. Tyson rode slumped in the saddle like a blanket Indian. His homely face wore a hangdog expression. His cockiness had vanished, and he was wallowing in self-pity. People in the street stopped to stare. Others gaped from the doorways and windows of houses and business places along the main street. Pete Amado came hurrying from the Mexican part of town, a fresh bandage about his head.

"That's the one, Will! He killed the *señora*!"

"Come along and tell that to the sheriff," Shannon said, dismounting. "Or did he ride out to look for the killers?"

Pete shook his head. "He can't ride out, because of a bad leg."

Sheriff Milt Owens's office had a door at the side of the two-storied building. The lawman sat at his rolltop desk, sideways to it, with his left leg propped up on a store box. The leg was in a plaster cast. A pair of crutches stood against the end of the desk. Owens was close to his three score and ten. He had grown gaunt and gray, wearing a star, but his china-blue eyes were still bright and alert.

He was apologetic. “Sorry I couldn’t ride out and give you a hand, Will. I stopped a slug up San Marcos way a week ago, chasing the Dolan brothers. It cracked a bone for me. But I figured that you, having been a lawman, wouldn’t really need me. It looks as though I figured right.” He shifted his gaze to the prisoner, his expression curdling. “This one sure doesn’t look like much. Still, it doesn’t take much of a man to pull a trigger.”

“This *bastardo* killed *Señora* Amhurst, Sheriff,” Pete Amado said. “I saw him fire the shot. I’ll swear to it in court.”

“You’ll get to do just that, Pete,” Owens said. “Now how about going around back to the jailhouse and fetching old Luke Givens so he can lock this jasper up?”

Pete nodded, but he didn’t leave on the errand at once. He stared at the scarecrowish prisoner with hatred. His leathery, pitted face worked with the intensity of his feelings. Pete seemed to want to kill Red Tyson with his bare hands. Sensing this, the youth moved so that Shannon was between him and the Mexican.

Shannon said, “Ease up, *amigo*. He’ll pay for what he’s done.”

Pete shook his head. “You shouldn’t have

brought him in, Will. You should have killed him."

He turned and left the office, muttering to himself.

"A terrible thing, two fine people like the Amhursts being murdered," Sheriff Owens said. "I can understand how old Pete feels. Why, Will? Why did it happen?"

"The kid here claims that the black man—Ben Murdock—bore Phil a grudge from away back," Shannon said. "Pete heard Murdock tell Phil that he'd been hunting him for more than a dozen years. It's hard to believe, but Phil Amhurst must have wronged him in some way. The kid, if he's telling the truth, was with the black man as a hired gun. He and a half-breed named Sanchez."

Owens put on a pair of silver-framed spectacles, reached for a ledger, and dipped a pen in the inkwell on the desk.

"I've got to book you, son. What's your name?"

"Red Tyson."

"What were you called before you got nicknamed Red?"

"Isaac. I don't like that name any."

"What you like or don't like won't matter anymore," the sheriff said, and entered the name in his ledger. He wrote more, saying the words aloud: "Held on suspicion of murder."

"You can't hang me," Tyson said. "I'm only fifteen."

"He's seventeen, Sheriff," Shannon said. "And I've told him that if the law doesn't hang him, I'll damn well . . ."

He fell silent, letting it ride.

Sheriff Owens pretended not to have heard the unfinished threat. "All right, Isaac," he said. "Why did you and your partners kill Mr. and Mrs. Amhurst? I can't believe you don't know."

"It was an accident, her getting killed. She had a shotgun and . . ."

Pete Amado came with Owens's deputy, Luke Givens, who wasn't quite as old as the sheriff but was well into senility. He had a look of fragility. His hair and moustache were snow white. To Shannon, he looked like a man with one foot in the grave. Luke served only as bailiff when court was in session and as jailer when there were prisoners. His feebleness worried Shannon.

When the sheriff told Givens to lock Red Tyson up, Shannon said, "Pete, you go along, just in case." He feared that the youth would jump the deputy and make a run for it.

When he was alone with Milt Owens, Shannon said, "Since you can't do any manhunting, I'll be going after the two others. How about making my going after them official by deputizing me?"

Without hesitating, Owens took a deputy sheriff's six-pointed star from a drawer of his desk and handed it to Shannon.

"Consider yourself sworn in, Will," he said.

"You realize, of course, that I wouldn't do this but for your past experience as a peace officer. I know you won't take that badge as a license to kill. Bring that black man and the half-breed in, if you can."

"I know how the law game is played, Sheriff," Shannon said, slipping the star into his shirt pocket. "I'll set out right after the funeral. Right now I'd better outfit for a long stay in the desert. I've a hunch those two will lead me a merry chase."

"Sorry I can't go with you."

"I'm sorry about that, too," Shannon said. "Because that Ben Murdock . . ."

He shook his head, figuring it was no use trying to explain what that black man was like.

He left the office, went to get breakfast at the Welcome Cafe, then busied himself with getting a pack outfit together.

The double funeral was held at two o'clock that afternoon, with the service conducted by the Reverend Eli Grubb. The business places were closed, and just about everybody in town, from the Mexican as well as the Anglo part, came to the cemetery. Phil and Kate Amhurst had been well liked indeed.

After his sister and brother-in-law had been laid to rest, Shannon went to McDade's Livery Stable. He had the hostler get the halter and packsaddle on the mule he had bought for the manhunt while he saddled his blue roan. He led the animals down the street to Phil's store. The provisions and camp gear he had bought from the clerk, Henry Yates, were piled on the porch, and he began loading them on the mule.

Henry came to lend a hand. He was a bald little man who peered owlishly at his small world through gold-rimmed spectacles. He had a habitually anxious look, and Phil had once told Shannon that this was because Mrs. Yates was a shrew who kept Henry henpecked. Nothing the man did pleased the lady. Today he seemed more nervous than usual. He kept fumbling and dropping the things he handed Shannon to pack away.

When the man let a package of Arbuckle coffee slip from his fingers, Shannon said, "What ails you? Are you all that upset about your boss and his wife?"

"It was a terrible shock, their getting murdered," Henry said. "Then there's the store. Martha—that's Mrs. Yates, you know—has been worrying whether or not it will be kept open, now that Mr. Amhurst is gone. She's scared I'll lose my job. And . . . well, I am, too."

Shannon had given the store not a single thought, but he could understand Henry's being concerned about it. Jobs were hard to find in Valido.

Henry went on, "Martha said I'm to ask you what's what, since it's up to you."

Shannon had everything loaded. He covered the pack with a tarpaulin, which he began lashing down with rope.

"What's up to me?" he asked, not much interested.

"Why, keeping the store open," Henry said. "It's yours now, isn't it?"

Shannon stared at him blankly. "Mine? How do you figure that?"

"Why, Mr. Amhurst made out a will soon after he married your sister. It left everything to her. I know, because he had me sign as a witness, along with Ed Hibley, the barber. And if it was like your hired hand told it, Mr. Amhurst was killed first. That means Mrs. Amhurst came into his estate for the few minutes before she was killed. And you as her next of kin inherit what was hers. You—"

"Quit it, Henry, for God's sake," Shannon exploded, losing his temper. "I don't want to hear about this, with Phil and Kate only just buried. Keep the store open. Take your salary out of the till. When I get back, we'll talk about it some more."

"Yes, sir, Mr. Shannon. That's a weight off my mind, believe me. Martha will feel better, too. I'll take care of everything for you. You can trust me, just like Mr. Amhurst did."

Shannon wasn't listening. He couldn't close

his ears, but he didn't let any more of what the clerk said register in his mind. He mounted the blue roan and took hold of the mule's lead rope. Seeing Pete Amado coming from one direction and Sheriff Owens from another, he waited impatiently for them to come up. He was eager to get on with the manhunt. Every minute he wasted here, Ben Murdock and Sanchez lengthened their lead.

Pete was wearing a new steeple-crowned straw sombrero on top of his bandages. He'd been drinking tequila, and he was less steady on his legs than the sheriff was on his crutches.

Pete took hold of the roan's bridle. "Wait, *compadre*," he said, hiccuping loudly. "I will get a horse and a gun, and ride with you. You will need me to side you."

"I'll need you to look after the ranch," Shannon told him. "Have your drunk today, but get back out there tomorrow." He looked at Sheriff Owens, who had joined them and was leaning awkwardly on his crutches. "Milt, you'll see that he pulls out in the morning?"

"I'll do that," Owens said, then he held out a pair of handcuffs that he'd pulled from his pocket. "For that black man, when you take him prisoner," he added. "They'll make him easier to bring in."

If I take him, Shannon thought, again remembering what Ben Murdock was like.

He dropped the handcuffs into a hip pocket.

"Well, *hasta luego*."

"Good hunting," the sheriff said.

And old Pete, hiccuping again, muttered, "*Vaya con Dios*."

Shannon smiled mirthlessly and rode out with the mule in tow. He would see them again when he saw them, and maybe he would have God on his side. Without a doubt he would need somebody or something siding him.

Shannon left Valido at the west end and reined in after crossing the creek bridge beyond the edge of the town. A cavalry detail was approaching from the northwest, and the officer had motioned for him to wait.

A shavetail lieutenant, the officer still had a boyish look. He was sprouting a moustache, doubtlessly to make him look more mature, but he didn't appear to be having much luck with it. His detail consisted of a sergeant, ten troopers, and two packhorses. They had been in the field for a while; men and mounts had lost their spit and polish. They were sweaty and dusty. The lieutenant himself had lost the ramrod West Point had given him for a spine.

"Sir, I wouldn't advise that you travel the west road," he said. "Delgado is out again. He left the reservation two nights ago with twenty-some Chiricahuas and Mescaleros, all well armed. They were last reported seen between here and

Tucson, but the Army has yet to make contact with them. All travelers are being advised to remain off the roads until the danger is past."

"I'm heading south, Lieutenant."

"Delgado could be in that direction by now."

Shannon brought out his badge and held it for the lieutenant to see. "I've pressing business. It won't keep."

"You realize what a risk you'll be running, don't you?"

"I do," Shannon said. "I'll keep my eyes open. Thanks for the warning."

Ben Murdock *and* a bunch of bronco Apaches, as if the black man weren't enough for him to worry about. Shannon rode on with these disquieting thoughts, soon leaving the road and striking out across the trackless desert.

Instead of going directly to the Frio Hills, where he would pick up the trail of Murdock and Sanchez, he swung over to the Harbolds' Rocker H ranch. This was the spread nearest his own, and the Harbold cattle shared the range with his stock. He had become close friends with Sam and Lily and their three nearly grown sons, and he'd had them on his mind since his encounter with the cavalry detail. Their place was as remote as his own, and word of Delgado's being on the prod might be slow in reaching them.

He rode into their yard shortly before sundown,

his arrival heralded by the frantic barking of their dog: a mongrel of uncertain ancestry and of almost as many colors as Joseph's coat. Lily appeared at the door and scolded the dog upon seeing the reason for its raising a fuss.

"Patches, stop it! Be quiet, I say!"

She smiled a welcome for Shannon.

"Will, how nice. Dad and the boys will be glad you stopped by. They'll be coming in for supper shortly. Get down and put up your horse." She looked wonderingly at his pack animal. "A mule, for heaven's sake, Will?"

A gray-haired, comfortably stout woman in a calico dress and an apron, she had a look of contentment that told of her total acceptance of life in this lonely place. She had her husband and her sons and no need for the rest of the world, except for an occasional visit to town.

"I won't be staying, Lily," Shannon told her. "I'm on my way down to the Frios. I stopped by to warn you folks that Delgado is on the loose again. The cavalry is after him, but as always rounding him up will take a while."

Lily's pleasant face became shadowed with concern. "Will there never be an end to this Apache trouble? I'll tell Sam and the boys, Will, and they'll stay close to home until that rascal is caught. Thanks for coming to warn us. You really won't stay to supper?"

Shannon shook his head. "I've no time to visit,

Lily." Then, bleak of face and voice, he told her why he had to be on his way.

She stared at him with shocked, incredulous eyes. "Phil and Kate dead . . . murdered? Oh, Will, how awful!"

"A hell of a thing, all right," he said. "And I've got to be after those two killers. I won't have any peace of mind until I get them."

"Alone, Will? You're going after them alone?"

"It's got to be alone. The sheriff is on crutches with a shot-up leg."

"Wait until Sam comes in. Maybe he . . ."

Shannon shook his head. "I wouldn't ask it of him. Not with a bunch of Apaches on the loose. He may be needed here." He lifted the reins and kneed the roan into motion. "See you folks when I get back, Lily."

"Take care, Will," Lily said. "Please take care."

He nodded and rode out. For a little while, for the time it took him to travel perhaps a mile, he thought of the Harbolds and of the good life they had in spite of the hardships and privations they endured. Sam and Lily were raising three sons who would do them proud, and each of those boys would one day marry and have children of his own. The Harbolds' Rocker H ranch would grow and prosper, and upon it a dynasty was being founded. That was achievement. It was the ultimate fulfillment.

Phil and Kate had realized that when they met.

They had taken great joy in the life coming into being through their union. Only at this moment did it occur to Shannon that Ben Murdock and his companions had taken not just two lives, they had destroyed a third as well: that of Kate's unborn child.

Shannon's hatred was already total. He could not hate more because of this realization; that was an impossibility. For a moment, in fact, his thoughts lay elsewhere. He considered his own lot and admitted that he did, as Phil Amhurst had said, lead a hermitlike existence. He had missed out on all that made a man's brief stay on earth worthwhile. Never having found a Kate or a Lily to share his life, he was in reality an incomplete man.

What am I, really?

Shaking himself mentally, he rid his mind of such disheartening thoughts and faced up to being a vengeance seeker. There existed for him now only two other human beings in all the world: the black man and the half-breed, each of whom must die on the gallows . . . or, yes, by his gun.

The day came to its end, but he continued on his way, not even stopping to cook and eat an evening meal. He had no appetite, he felt no hunger. Hatred nourished him. Dusk gathered, thickened into darkness. A nearly full moon rose from behind the eastern mountains. It was blood red in color. He wondered if Ben Murdock too watched the ruddily luminous disk. His state of mind was such that he could think of nothing but Murdock. The half-breed Sanchez did not loom important in his mind. He was becoming obsessed with the giant black man.

CHAPTER FOUR

Preoccupied though he was with thinking of the black man, Shannon did not forget that the bloodthirsty Delgado had once more jumped the reservation. He rode warily, stopping frequently to listen for the sounds of horses, Indian ponies, in motion. He knew that Apaches seldom launched an attack at night, holding as they did the superstitious belief that the spirits of warriors slain during the hours of darkness would be denied the sanctuary of the spirit world. But Delgado's band might be on the move, and he did not want to blunder into it. Darkness or no darkness, they might well jump a lone white man.

He heard nothing to alarm him. The only sounds were those of the desert's nocturnal creatures: the squeaking of bats, the hooting of an occasional owl, the sharp cry of a nighthawk, the howling duet of a pair of coyotes. He traveled at a brisk walk, and, in the hour before dawn, when the night seemed its darkest, he came to the first rocky heights of the Frios. He ventured no farther, for the Apaches knew of the well in the gorge and there was the long chance that they had made their night camp by it.

He pulled in close to the base of a cliff, among a jumble of rocks, and staked the animals out after unsaddling one and removing the pack from the other. He rationed water from his canteen, letting the horse and mule drink in turn from the canvas bucket he'd packed along. He drank sparingly, then smoked a cigarette while hunkered down with his back to a boulder. Finally he wrapped himself in his blankets and slept until daylight woke him.

He climbed a rocky knob of ground and scanned the area for coppery-skinned horsemen, but he saw no moving thing in all that immensity of space. He returned to his camp, got his animals under saddle and pack, and headed for the gorge where the abandoned diggings were located.

He rode slowly, cutting for signs. He saw only the tracks of shod hooves, those that had been made by his own horse and by the mounts of the murderers. No Indian ponies had been through here recently. He swung over to the well and dismounted. Taking the canvas bucket from one of the mule's packsaddle pockets, he tied the end of his rope to its bail. He lowered the bucket into the well, intending to give his animals a full watering. It struck some obstacle that kept it from reaching the water.

Looking down, he swore with flaring rage. The obstacle was a dead calf, its rump end protruding from the water. He hauled the bucket up empty, damning Ben Murdock to the torments of everlasting hell. The black man must have spent a good part of yesterday finding that calf out on the range, maybe miles away, driving it here and shooting it. He could visualize Murdock picking up the carcass and dumping it down into the well, laughing his unholy laughter at the grim joke he was playing on Will Shannon.

But the man had gone to the bother for more reason than to get his goat, Shannon knew. He had wanted to pollute the well so his pursuer could not use the water. He had known that horses would drink nothing that was fouled by blood.

He figured I wouldn't know of any other water close by and would have to turn back. Hell, he should know me better than all that by now.

Shannon put the bucket away, mounted the roan, took the mule in tow, and rode on through the gorge. He could and would do this: let Murdock and Sanchez lead him to water.

He had the tracks of not two but three horses to follow. Like himself, the two murderers were traveling with a pack animal. The hoof marks led him out of the Frios on their south side and then west across the desert. Of the men and horses making those tracks he saw nothing, even in the far distance.

The sun climbed in the pale, cloudless sky, burning the already sere earth with its hot glare. Heat haze shimmered on every rise or cluster of rocks. Dust devils appeared here and there; they had their brief frolic, then vanished. The spiky growth gave way to sand flats. The dunes reflected the sunlight, and here the air was oven hot. Hunger came to Shannon, but his thirst was greater. He and his animals were becoming dehydrated. After he had stopped and drunk sparingly from his canteen, he divided the remaining water between the horse and mule. They craved more. So did he. His thirst was torment. Suffering a momentary dizziness, he realized that he was weakening because his system was being wrung dry of moisture. Starting out again, he walked and led the animals. The roan was faltering, the mule growing balky.

Must find water, soon.

The thought was fuzzy, for his mind functioned sluggishly. His vision kept blurring. His mouth was cottony, his lips parched. He found himself wondering what the temperature might be. For some unfathomable reason, it seemed important that he know. His guess was that here in the *malpais*, the wasteland, a thermometer would register ten or more degrees above the one hundred mark.

Ahead rose a range of those humpy mountains peculiar to southern Arizona, and his quarry's tracks, now leading southwest, told him that the pair had swung around the end of it. Four or five miles from these mountains the terrain changed again. The barren sand flats gave way to a long, gradual slope dense with greasewood, chollas, and towering saguaro cacti. He saw a moving thing midway up the grade. He pulled up short, reaching for his rifle. By staring fixedly, he made out a Longhorn cow. Shortly he spotted two other such creatures. Hope came alive in him. Where cattle lived, there must be water. He flipped a mental coin and immediately abandoned the tracks of Murdock and Sanchez to make his way up the slope. The gradient was a steeper incline than it had appeared to his uncertain sight, and soon he was lurching and staggering on wobbly legs. The horse and mule tried to pull away from him, and he realized that they had caught the scent of water.

He hauled himself to the roan's back, with great effort, then let the animal have its head. Within half a mile the animals brought him to a stream that flowed down from the foothills beyond. It was only a few inches deep and barely a yard wide, but to Shannon, and to his animals, it was a godsend. They plunged their muzzles into it, and he, all but collapsing as he left the saddle, lay flat and drank greedily with them. He removed his hat and splashed water against his face. With his cupped hands, he poured water over his head and down the back of his neck. He felt his strength begin to return, and with it came hunger.

He pulled the horse and mule away from the stream, for they were drinking too much. They were glutting themselves, becoming bloated. He removed their rigging, then staked them out on the grass that grew thickly about the creek. He gathered dead brush, kindled a fire, and filled his small coffee pot. While the coffee brewed, he sliced bacon into the frying pan and mixed batter for flapjacks. He cooked and ate this poor fare with relish, then smoked a cigarette, and afterward settled down to sleep.

Waking three hours later, he made a fresh fire and cooked another meal. After eating this time, he let the animals drink again. Then he readied them for the trail. He filled his canteen and rode out, an hour later picking up his quarry's trail once more.

He followed the tracks past the end of the mountain range. The hoof marks gave him a sense of nearness to the men he was trailing, but he knew he was deluding himself. He was not close to them. He had not cut down their lead to any considerable extent, if at all. To shorten it, to overtake them, he would have to keep on the move throughout the approaching night.

That thought was still in his mind when he saw smoke rising from some craggy bluffs a short distance to the south. It rose blackly against the sky in a series of puffs. Smoke signals. Apache smoke signals, certainly. He'd all but forgotten Delgado. And a forgetful man, with Delgado on the loose, could lose his scalp, his life. He reined in, looking one way and another for answering smoke signals. He saw no smoke elsewhere, but he knew that didn't necessarily mean that there weren't Apaches ahead of him or behind him as well as at the bluffs.

What the hell were they signaling?

That a white man was coming along with a laden mule in tow? A lone white man whose scalp might easily be lifted?

That was a possibility he couldn't ignore. He looked about for a place where he could have cover and make a stand. Seeing no such place nearby, he turned toward the base of the closest mountain slope. He ran the horse and the mule, caught up by a sense of urgency. The ground rose sharply now, and he was again riding through dense brush and among tall saguaro cacti. He pulled up at the base of the mountain slope, dismounted, and tied the animals to the skeleton of a dead saguaro. He pulled his rifle from its boot, then had another look toward the range of bluffs. He'd made his move none too soon. The Apaches were on their way.

Two came riding from the bluffs, and three others were approaching from the west. Odds of five to one. Not good, and yet not impossible. He looked for cover and saw a dry wash running southeastward down the brush-grown grade. He dropped into this broad ditch and, crouching low, moved along it until he was about two hundred yards from where he had left the horse and mule.

Keeping down so he was unseen by the Indians, he was unable to watch their approach. Long minutes passed, and then, failing to hear them riding up the grade, he raised his head and looked downward, and almost missed seeing them. They had left their ponies below and climbed on foot. They were already above him, moving through the brush as silently as shadows.

Four were naked except for breechclouts, boot-type moccasins, headbands, and bandoliers of cartridges. The fifth wore a battered old top hat and a red miner's shirt. Each was armed with a rifle. They came within sight of his animals and stopped to look about for him. Failing to see him, they remained as still as copper statues for a long moment. They then looked at each other in perplexity and perhaps alarm.

Shannon lined his rifle on the top-hatted warrior. The Apache must have sensed danger, for he spun about and stared directly at Shannon. He was not a young man. His face beneath the ludicrous hat was ancient and wizened. The gazes of the two men met and locked. The eyes of the Indian were like shiny black glass beads. His black-copper face contorted with hatred. He opened his mouth and let out a wild yell. Instantly all five of the Apaches were in motion. They charged at Shannon, howling like demons and firing their rifles.

Shannon held his fire until he was sure he would not miss, thinking them foolhardy rather than brave. They were placing too much trust in the odds being with them. He began firing slowly and methodically. He shot the warrior with the hat dead center in the chest. As that one went down, he jacked another cartridge into the Winchester's chamber and lined his sights on the next nearest buck. This second warrior went down with an unholy yell. The third leapt high in the air when hit, making no outcry. He dropped loosely, sprawling in a grotesquely twisted posture and not moving again. The remaining two decided that their medicine had failed. They stopped shooting and swerved away in abrupt flight. They fled wildly down the grade, and a moment later Shannon heard the drumming of hooves as they raced away on their ponies.

A haze of gray powder smoke hung in the still air about Shannon. He had the stink of it in his nostrils, the taste of it in his mouth. This was not something he liked. Nor did he like having had to shoot down the three bucks sprawled out there. One of them was still alive. It was the warrior who had cried out when hit. He began crawling away, leaving his rifle behind and leaking blood. Shannon beaded him for another shot, then shook his head and lowered his rifle.

After dragging himself along for perhaps a hundred yards, the Apache struggled to his feet and continued downward at a limping walk. He mounted his pony and rode slowly after the two others who had fled. They were heading toward the bluffs from which the smoke signals had risen.

Shannon had no feeling that he was in the clear. The cavalry officer had said that Delgado had jumped the reservation with twenty-some warriors. Fifteen or more were somewhere around, almost certainly in this immediate area. But in which direction? Shannon didn't bother to guess that as he returned to his horse and mule. The tracks he followed led west, and west he would go, Apaches or no Apaches.

He too took flight, striking out at a hard run. After traveling for perhaps a mile, he looked back over his shoulder. He was not being pursued, and no more smoke signals rose from the bluffs. He began to breathe more easily. He slowed the roan and mule to a walk and cut for the murderers' sign again. He found their tracks shortly, and they still led west. He followed them toward the setting sun, which blazed redly as it slid toward the far mountains.

Shannon kept on the move with the coming of night, counting upon being able to pick up the trail again in the morning. His need now was to get out of this Apache-infested area and to shorten the murderers' lead. He held the belief that Murdock and Sanchez would continue to travel westward, with Yuma their destination. According to Red Tyson, the black man had a diggings up the Colorado River from that grubby town at the far edge of the Territory. If unable to cut the sign of his quarry with daylight, Shannon told himself, he would head for that place. The prospect of such a trip was not to his liking, however. The farther west a man rode the more tortuous the desert became.

He stopped for an hour in the middle of the night to rest the animals, and at dawn he made camp in a broad hollow where there were grass and a water hole. He built a fire, cooked and ate breakfast, then took his rifle and climbed a hump of ground that offered a view of the area in every direction.

To the west by about five miles was another mountain range with the usual knobby, saguaro-studded foothills at its base. Between his position and the hills lay another stretch of *malpais*. This was a vast area of rock: of jumbled, piled boulders and stone slabs. It had a forbidding look; it was a maze through which a rider would be forced to travel slowly. He would need water again, with the coming of the new day's heat. He doubted that any was to be found out there.

He saw no riders in any direction, and so he settled down to sleep for a couple of hours. Some giant rocks crowned the rise, and he settled himself among them. He merely catnapped, waking often. Finally some sound roused him completely. He rose and looked about. Seeing nothing, no one, he let a puzzled frown come to his leathery face. In his perplexity, he rubbed a hand over his bristly chin. He *had* heard something. He hadn't been sleeping so soundly that he would have dreamed that sound. His animals were safe in the hollow, grazing placidly. Whatever the sound had been, it had not frightened either the blue roan or the mule. An edginess got hold of him. Worry filled his mind. He had not panicked when the five Apaches charged him, but the unseen had him in a state of alarm.

Then he heard gunfire. The sound came to him from a distance; from deep within the rock field, he decided. The racketing of rifles ceased after a minute or two, then a single weapon began shooting at lengthy intervals, as though the man using it was laying down a sniping fire. This rifle's reports were heavier than the sharp cracks of the ubiquitous Winchester.

A buffalo gun, Shannon thought. *The black man's Sharps!*

Murdock and Sanchez had run into Delgado's main band, certainly. And Murdock at least was still alive. Since the Apache rifles were now silent, the black man must have driven them back with his far-reaching weapon. But even as Shannon had that thought the other rifles began shooting again, so many of them that he was unable to guess at their number. The shooting continued for several minutes, then ceased abruptly. The buffalo gun too was silent now.

They did for him . . . he's a goner.

Somehow Shannon felt cheated. The Apaches had robbed him of his revenge.

CHAPTER FIVE

After perhaps an hour Shannon saw the Apaches emerge from the rock jungle, appearing a short distance to the south of his vantage point. He crouched among the boulders atop the rise and watched them intently, trying to will them to pass by without becoming aware of his presence.

Fourteen of them, one doubtlessly the long-time blood enemy of the white man, Delgado. They were hazing five riderless horses along with them. Two of these animals carried saddles and had probably belonged to Murdock and Sanchez. Yes, one of the saddled horses was a big black: Ben Murdock's mount.

Fourteen squat-bodied, coppery-skinned horse-men of the desert, as tough organisms as ever took human form. Fierce fighters, infinitely cruel in victory and unwilling to accept the defeat that had come to them after two hundred years of warfare waged against them first by the Spaniards, then by the Mexicans, and finally by the Americans. The Apache . . . the Enemy.

They passed on, and Shannon's heart slowed from its hard, excited pounding. They vanished over the eastern rim of the desert, and his taut nerves relaxed. He felt that he had much to be thankful for at this moment. He would have put up a fight if they had seen and attacked him, but he couldn't have survived a battle with that swarm of warriors.

He returned to the hollow and readied the roan and mule for the trail once more. He let them drink again, and they drank the water hole dry. Riding out, he headed westward again. Because of the Apaches, he did not dare ride east, directly toward Valido. He did want to enter the rock field, for he needed to see the bodies of the murderers. He had to know beyond all doubt that the two were dead.

He located the scene of the fighting easily enough by backtracking the Apaches. This was deep in the wasteland, at a *tinaja*, a rock-bound spring and pool, about which lay scattered, over a wide area, seven slain warriors and five dead horses. One of the latter was burdened with a pack, and he knew it for his quarry's animal.

Shannon searched all about and far from the *tinaja* but found neither Murdock nor Sanchez. He had to accept the incredible, the seemingly impossible: the black man and his companion had survived the fighting and escaped on foot, after bringing down seven of their attackers. Shannon felt a sudden, grudging respect for the pair, or at least for Ben Murdock. It would have been the black man's buffalo gun that had done the trick.

Puzzled as to how Murdock had managed it,

Shannon returned to the *tinaja.* A mass of huge rock slabs, piled one atop the other, rose to a height of fifty feet. He dismounted and began to climb this gigantic heap. He found that it was cut through with crevices that could serve a man as passageways and permit him to move from side to side and from level to level. He followed one of the passageways and near the top of the rock mound found where Murdock and Sanchez had made their stand. Here, in a shallow space about eight feet in diameter, was a litter of spent cartridge brass.

Years ago Shannon had served in the Texas Rangers with a former Johnny Reb who had been at Gettysburg during the War. This man had told him of having been one of the Confederate sharpshooters who had made a massive pile of rocks called Devil's Den into a hornets' nest for the Yankees during that battle. Murdock and Sanchez had made this as deadly a spot for the Apaches. Fully protected, they had been able to lay down a fire heavy enough to give Delgado and his braves a bellyful of fighting. When the Indians had withdrawn, badly hurt, the black man and his companion had simply walked away. But they'd been set afoot. Shannon's glum, stubbly face suddenly lighted with a grin of anticipation.

By damn, I've got them!

They'd lost not only their horses but also their provisions and camp gear. They were in a bad way. With him so close behind them, they were even worse off than they knew.

Shannon hurried down from the rocks, driven by a sense of urgency. He was eager for the showdown with the pair. When mounted, he rode a wide circle around the *tinaja.* He soon came upon two sets of boot tracks. The murderers were again heading west. He set out in the same direction, not bothering now to stay directly on the trail. He knew where they were headed; he didn't need to track them every inch of the way.

An hour later he broke out of the rocks onto a grassy mesa and saw a moving shape far across this tableland. One man, not two. Alarm touched him, for the thought came to him that the pair had split up and he now had one man ahead of him and one behind. He shot an anxious glance back over his shoulder but saw no one coming after him. Riding toward the man he had in sight, he soon saw that it was two men, one carrying the other piggyback: Murdock carrying Sanchez.

Better and better . . . for me, Shannon thought with a grim sort of satisfaction.

The half-breed had been wounded fighting the Apaches, and the black man had decided not to abandon him. Why he'd made such a decision, Shannon didn't try to guess. He had become convinced that there was no understanding Ben Murdock.

He was rapidly overtaking Murdock, and the

big man finally became aware of him. Coming to an abrupt halt and facing around, Murdock lowered his burden to the ground. He carried his buffalo gun in his right hand and had a canteen slung by its strap from his left shoulder. With his left hand Murdock removed his hat and with his shirt sleeve wiped sweat from his face.

Shannon reined in his roan horse and dropped the mule's lead rope. He took the deputy sheriff's badge from his pocket and pinned it to his shirt front. He drew his rifle from its boot and dismounted. Leaving his animals, he walked toward the two men. Sanchez lay unmoving at Murdock's feet. His shirt was stained red brown with dried blood. Evidently his wound had stopped bleeding. A burly sort, he must have been a tiring burden even for a man of Murdock's size and strength.

Murdock looked tired. He also looked dispirited. His great shoulders sagged, and he breathed laboriously through his slackly open mouth. His gold tooth glinted. The jagged scar across his left cheek stood out starkly, marring what was otherwise a handsome face. He gazed dull eyed at Shannon, making no hostile move with the Sharps rifle. It no longer gave him the edge. He had let Shannon come too close. The Winchester repeater was now more than a match for the buffalo gun.

"I figured you'd be coming, boss, but not

this soon," he said. "How'd you get past them Apaches?"

"You're under arrest, Murdock," Shannon said. "You'd better submit, because if you don't I'll damn well kill you without it bothering me any. Now drop that rifle. And shuck your gun rig."

"You can kill me, all right," Murdock said. "But you'll have to shoot me in the back to do it."

He turned and started walking away.

Over his shoulder he said, "Come after me when you've done what you can for the breed; then we'll see who kills who."

Shannon drove a shot after him. It was an intentional near miss. Murdock kept on walking.

"Listen, damn you!" Shannon shouted. "Pull up or I'll put a slug through your leg!"

Murdock did not stop, and Shannon, not having it in him to carry out his threat, cursed his own soft-heartedness as he had done that day he'd been unable to kill the buck deer. He went to Sanchez, bent over him briefly, then again shouted at the black man.

"Tell me this, you . . . Why were you packing a dead man?"

That brought Murdock facing about.

"The breed's dead?" He shook his head sorrowfully. "Too bad. I'd hoped he had a chance."

Shannon stared at him bewilderedly. "I don't savvy you, black man. You left Red Tyson for me to kill or take in to be hanged, but you wouldn't leave this one to shift for himself when he got hit. Why?"

"I'll tell you why, mister. That kid shot the woman after I told him not to do it. Even aside from that he wasn't worth a damn. He was born mean. He was always itching to use his gun on somebody."

"He was your man. You hired him."

"When I pay a man wages, I expect him to take orders from me," Murdock said. "As for Sanchez, he wasn't a bad hombre. I had nothing against him. Like me, he just had the bad luck not to be born with lily white skin."

"Feeling that way, you owe it to him to bury him. You can't leave him here for the buzzards, can you?"

"Reckon I can't," Murdock said after a lengthy silence. "But I ain't such a fool that I'll start digging a grave so you can jump me. It's a Mexican standoff, Shannon. You haven't got the edge, and neither have I. You ain't the kind to shoot a man in the back, and I ain't aiming to kill you unless you try to take me. You give me your word that you won't jump me while I'm burying the breed?"

"You'd take my word for that?"

"I figure I savvy what kind of a hombre you are."

"All right. You've got my word. We'll bury

him, then go back to a Mexican standoff. After that I'll figure out how to take you . . . to be hanged along with that fool kid."

Murdock laid his rifle and canteen on the ground.

As he walked toward Shannon, he said, "I get to pick up my buffalo gun afterward. And I'm keeping my six-shooter belted on." He smiled wryly. "I don't trust any white man all the way. You got something to dig with?"

"Only an ax and a frying pan."

"They'll do," Murdock said.

They worked together at opening a grave for the half-breed. Murdock used Shannon's short-handled ax to break the ground, and Shannon used his skillet and at times his bare hands to scoop out the loosened earth. They struck caliche, soil almost as hard as concrete, at a depth of three feet and could not penetrate it with such makeshift tools.

"This will have to do for him," Shannon said.

They wrapped the dead man in one of Shannon's blankets and laid him in the shallow grave, then pushed the soil in on top of him. No prayers were said, no tears shed, but Murdock looked downcast. Shannon brought out makings and made a cigarette for himself, afterward offering the tobacco and papers to the black man. Murdock accepted them. They hunkered down side by side to have their smoke.

After a minute or two Shannon said, "What wrong did Phil Amhurst do you?"

Grimacing, Murdock said, "He's dead. Let's forget him."

Shannon shook his head. "I can't forget him. He was my brother-in-law. I was fond of him, and I thought well of him. It couldn't have been such a big wrong that you had to kill him after more than a dozen years. No matter what, a man can't keep on hating that long."

"I can, and I did," Murdock said. "All right, since you've got to know how that bastard wronged me. . . . Back after the War I was set free like the rest of the slaves. I was luckier than most, because I had a decent man for a master. And because I'd been more than a field hand working under an overseer's whip. I had a knack for fixing and making things. There wasn't anything I couldn't turn a hand to.

"I was a carpenter, a stonemason, a bricklayer, a blacksmith, a tinsmith, a shoemaker. Anything that needed doing, I could do it. I was like that as a kid. Seeing it, my master had the tutor he hired for his children teach me numbers and how to figure. It was against the law, but young Master Charles, the tutor, got me to learn the alphabet and showed me how to read too. So by the time I was grown I could figure out measurements, like a man working at any trade needs to do."

Murdock's deep, rich voice had taken on a

huskiness. He seemed caught up by nostalgia. Shannon had the impression that his memories of his early life were not entirely unpleasant.

"My master even hired me out to build and repair things," the black man continued. "He made money off me that way. Then, after the War, my master was poor. He couldn't pay wages to us slaves that Mr. Lincoln had set free. He had to tell us to go. Me . . . he gave me a little stake. Eighty dollars. And he told me to get out of Mississippi, where there were too many freed slaves, all looking for work and going hungry because they couldn't find any."

Murdock fell silent and seemed lost in gloomy thought. He was a man of about forty, Shannon reckoned. He'd laid aside his hat while working on the grave, and a few gray hairs could be seen in his kinky black thatch. As Shannon had noted before, Ben Murdock was handsome in the negroid way. A lamentable thing, that ugly scar across his left cheek. It gave his face a sinister cast. Shannon had the thought that most people would be repelled by the man because of the scar, his blackness, and his great size. Shannon's own reaction to him at the moment was quite different. He hadn't forgotten that Murdock had taken the lives of Phil and Kate and their unborn child, but he sensed that here was a human being of basically decent instincts. He felt that Ben Murdock was a kindly person, even a gentle one.

He had proof of his decency, he realized. The man could have killed him if he had wanted, first back at Slash S ranch and then again in the Frio Hills when he'd shot his hat off the boulder.

"I wasn't alone, back then," Murdock said. "I had a family: a wife and a little boy. I went to East Texas with them. I got us a homestead. I built a cabin and plowed the land. Besides farming, I did odd jobs for the white folks living neighbors to me. I even took work in the town that was about ten miles away, when I could get it. For a little while, about a year, we made out all right. Then the slave stealers came."

"Slave stealers?" Shannon said. "After the War?"

Murdock's face turned bleak, his voice bitter. "They were stealing free blacks then, but us niggers what lived in those parts called them slave stealers. Some white folks did, too. I got a job building a house in town. It was a far piece, and I didn't get home excepting over Sundays. One Saturday night I got home and my family was gone. I looked everywhere for them but couldn't find a single trace. Then some neighbors, white folks, told me my wife and boy had been carried off by strange men. I rode my mule back to town, whipping him the whole way. The sheriff said he'd try to get my family back but he didn't have much hope that he could. He told me the slave stealers took the people they carried off far away and put them on ships that went to Brazil. You ever hear of that country, Shannon?"

Nodding, Shannon said, "It's in South America."

"Down there, they still had black people in slavery. That's where my wife and son were taken, to be sold as slaves all over again. The sheriff didn't get them back for me. Neither did the soldiers, when I went to the fort. The officer told me the Army knew about the stealing and was trying to stop it. But the ships put in at Matamoros, across in Mexico, and the military couldn't do anything about them.

"I set out for Matamoros, hoping I'd be in time. I stole a boat at Brownsville and rowed across the Rio Grande. I talked to the *alcalde*, the mayor, and paid him what little money I had. He told me that a ship—*Cynthia Logan*, it was named—had sailed two days before with a cargo of niggers. And he told me the name of the boss man of the slave stealers: *Señor* Amhurst. And this *Señor* Amhurst lived in Matamoros, in a big, fine house."

Shannon's bristly, rough-hewn face held an expression of disbelief. Phil Amhurst had stolen and sold human beings? The Phil Amhurst of whom he had held such a high opinion? He had to believe it. He knew that Ben Murdock could not have invented such a tale as he was telling in a voice harsh with bitterness.

"You went to that big, fine house, did you?"

Murdock nodded. "I went to it. Amhurst had gunhands guarding him. They grabbed me and took me to him. He was a young man, handsome. He looked like a fine gentleman. But he taunted me, laughed at me. He admitted having carried off a woman and a small boy from a farm in my part of East Texas. They'd gone on the *Cynthia Logan.* Then he said, 'Maybe you'll get to see them again when *you* get to Brazil, nigger.' He told his gunhands to lock me up until the next ship came to take on more stolen people."

Murdock ran the forefinger of his left hand over his scar. His hands were enormous but in no way clumsy. Shannon could well believe that the black man was dexterous in the use of tools. He could visualize him working with a carpenter's hammer and saw or with a shoemaker's needle and awl with equal skill.

"I put up a fight," Murdock went on. "I knocked one of the gunhands down. I grabbed the other one up and threw him halfway across the room at their boss. I ran from the room and tried to get out of the house. But there were more gunhands. Too many more. They beat me to the floor with their guns and dragged me back to Amhurst. He was fit to be tied, a crazy man. He got the poker from the fireplace and hit me with it while the others held me. It had a hook at the end. The hook dug into my cheek and tore it open."

He stared belligerently at Shannon.

"You're not believing any of this about Phil Amhurst, are you?"

"I don't want to believe it, but I have to."

"It's the truth, so help me God. Every word."

"How did you get away from him and his gunhands?" Shannon asked, his curiosity whetted.

"They locked me in the cellar, but I busted out one night. I had to half kill one of the gunhands to get away. I went back to Texas, then set out for Mississippi. I went to see my old master, hoofing it the whole way. I told him what had happened and asked him to try to get my woman and young one back. He did try. Like I said, he was a decent master. He wrote a batch of letters. One to the American consul down there in Brazil. More than one to big, important people in Washington. It was four months before a letter came back from Brazil. The consulate wrote that the ship *Cynthia Logan* never made port. It sank at sea, and only the officers and crew members were saved. More than a hundred black people went down with it, among them my Lucy and little Abe."

Murdock ground his cigarette into the dust and rose. "You still aiming to take me in for the law to hang?"

Shannon, too, disposed of his cigarette and stood.

"I'm still of the same mind," he said. "I won't be taking you in for Phil Amhurst's murder now, but only for that of my sister. And for that of the child she was carrying inside her." His voice turned harsh. "You figure I should be satisfied with having Red Tyson, but that's twisted thinking. That kid was your hired hand, which means he was acting for you. You're as guilty as he is. Damn it, Murdock; you made a big mistake when you took him and the breed on. You could have done for Phil Amhurst on your own."

"I didn't know but what he still had gunhands guarding him. I figured I'd need Red and Sanchez. When I heard that Amhurst was living at Valido, I didn't hear that he was leading a decent, respectable life. I didn't give a thought to his maybe having changed. Mostly, men don't change. They end up the way they start out. I counted on his being up to something as bad as slave stealing, with gunhands still guarding him."

He picked up his hat and set it squarely on his woolly head. He stood with his big feet wide apart and his thumbs hooked in the cartridge-studded belt of his gun rig. Whether he intended it to be or not, this was the gunfighter's stance. He'd be good—deadly—with a six-shooter, Shannon had no doubt.

"I'm mighty sorry about your sister, white man," Murdock said, using a curt, hard tone. "All the more sorry because she was with child. But I'm not taking the blame for her and the child getting killed. I told that loco kid not to shoot her. Anyway, you see it one way and I see it another.

So I guess one of us will end up dead out here in the middle of nowhere. And I won't let it be me."

He turned and started away, then stopped and faced Shannon again.

"A strange thing, Shannon . . . I didn't feel any better after killing that no-good ofay. All those years of hating him and living only for the chance to find and kill him. I never stopped looking for him except when I had to scratch for money to live on. I thought that once I did for him I'd feel like the man I was during the little while I had my farm and my family. But I ain't feeling good at all. And you, Shannon . . . you wouldn't feel any better if you could take me for hanging. You know what the Good Book says?"

"I know," Shannon said. " 'Vengeance is mine . . . saith the Lord.' "

"Why don't you hold to that?"

"For the same reason you didn't. I figure that a man who does wrong here on earth should pay for it here on earth so it's certain that he does pay. You made Phil Amhurst pay for taking your wife and son, and I'm going to make you pay for the killing of my sister and her child."

Murdock shook his head, his expression again sorrowful.

"Boss, I had a liking for only one white man in all my life. That was my old master. But I could have one for you. You're a lot like him: a decent sort for an ofay, but mule stubborn. I'm going to feel real bad when you force me to kill you."

Again he started away.

Shannon called after him, "You haven't a chance, black man. Afoot and without grub, you can't get away from me. I'll nail you before this time tomorrow. So be sensible: give up."

Murdock raised his right arm to signal that he'd heard. He strode on to where his rifle and canteen lay. He picked them up, hanging the canteen from his left shoulder and holding the big, octagonal-barreled weapon in his right hand. Shannon went to where his rifle lay and picked it up.

"Mexican standoff again," Murdock called to him. "Nobody's got the edge right now. But there ain't no truce any more. A man can do what he figures he must. Too bad, boss."

Shannon took warning from that and was not caught completely off guard when, after half a dozen more strides, the black man whipped about and raised his rifle to his shoulder. He dropped to a prone shooting position, but Murdock fired before he got his sights lined on him. The report of the Sharps was followed by a commotion behind him. Looking around, he saw the blue roan collapsing. Blood spurted from its mouth and nostrils. Another shot from the buffalo gun, and the mule snorted, shuddered, and fell onto its left side.

"Now we're both afoot, boss!"

With that shouted taunt, Ben Murdock turned

and began to run. Shannon's hatred for him returned full force. Cursing him, he opened fire at his broad back. He drove half a dozen slugs after him, but none found its mark. The black man continued to run even though already out of rifle range. He was still running when he crested a rise of ground and then was gone from Shannon's sight.

CHAPTER SIX

Life as Will Shannon knew it was mostly a matter of two steps forward and then one backward. Even the single step gained brought a man its share of hard knocks. Having survived under such conditions, on one frontier or another, he knew better than to give in to despair. He took stock instead and found that he held an advantage over Ben Murdock. The black man had lost his provisions, and he had not.

We'll see whose strength holds out longer, black man!

He strode to where his mule and blue roan horse lay dead. The sight of them brought on a flare-up of anger, and he cursed Murdock for his wanton killing of the animals. Then he reflected that the man could have shot him instead. But his anger held.

Quit doing me favors, Murdock; because I'll be damned before I do you any.

From the roan's saddle he took the canteen, saddlebags, war bag, and the mate to the blanket in which they'd buried Sanchez. From the mule's pack he took the coffee pot and frying pan, stowing them away in the saddlebags. Into the bags he also packed as much of the provisions—flour, beans, jerky, bacon, coffee, and salt—as they would hold. The remainder he scattered on the ground, kicking dirt into it. If Murdock planned to circle back after nightfall and help himself, he would have slim pickings.

Shannon wanted him to go hungry. He wanted Ben Murdock weakened by hunger. That wouldn't take long, he figured. A man of such an enormous physique would need grub in quantity to keep up his strength. Yes, let the tricky bastard go hungry!

Shannon shouldered his saddlebags, war bag, and rolled blanket, picked up his canteen and rifle, and set out in the direction Murdock had taken. When he reached the crest of the rise where he had last seen the man, he peered into the sun-drenched distance but failed to spot him. He had boot marks to follow, however. Tricky though the black man was, he could not keep from leaving telltale signs.

During the remainder of the day Shannon followed those marks left by Murdock's oversized boots. He could tell by the tracks that his quarry was moving along briskly. The distance between the track of the left boot and that of the right was considerable, showing that Murdock was taking long, strong strides. Shannon forced himself to do the same. Despite the punishing desert heat, he did no lagging. He suffered boots that began to pinch and bore the ache that came to leg muscles unused to walking. He drank frequently but sparingly from his canteen, so that *his* strength would not be sapped. He felt no need to ration his water supply to the point of denial. Somehow he knew that Murdock would lead him to water.

At sundown the boot tracks led him into a maze of foothills. Here the saguaro cacti grew forest dense, studding the hills and the lower portion of the mountain slopes beyond. This form of desert growth, which grew to twenty feet and more in height, liked hilly country. It never thrived where the land was flat. Dusk came, thickening swiftly into darkness. No longer able to read signs, Shannon stopped for the night.

Tired to the core, he dropped his gear and sank to the ground. Removing his boots and socks, he found his feet blistered in several spots and rubbed raw in one place. In his weariness he decided to forego a fire and a cooked meal. He dug a strip of jerky from the saddlebags and bit off a piece of the tough dried beef. He made it chewable by taking an occasional small sip of water.

After this skimpy meal he rolled and lit a cigarette. While having his smoke, he took a box of cartridges from the saddlebags and slipped as many loads into his Winchester as its magazine would hold. The remainder of the cartridges he put in his pockets. His Colt's revolver was fully loaded, except for the chamber under the hammer. That chamber was left empty for the sake of safety. Five loads in the revolver were enough anyway, to his way of thinking. He favored a rifle over a handgun, having more faith in its accuracy.

His cigarette smoked, he stubbed it out and rolled himself up in his blanket. He had no feeling that the black man was anywhere near, and he let himself drift off into a sound sleep.

Waking in the gray dawn, he built a fire, cooked breakfast, and ate hurriedly. He set out on Murdock's trail before the sun appeared, when the eastern sky was still a mottled pink and gold.

The trail led on through the foothills and down a long slope toward a gap in the mountains. The sun was up now, a fiery red disk. Its heavy heat had already dissipated the lingering night coldness. The gap led into a vast canyon, and once he was within the gorge Shannon came to a small creek that flowed a meandering course along its bottom. He stopped to drink and refill his canteen, seeing by the tracks that Murdock had slaked his thirst at this same spot.

The canyon widened farther on, and its steep, saguaro-studded slopes became higher. Its floor was dense with brush, and along the swift-flowing stream there grew paloverde, ironwood, mesquite, and other varieties of trees. With the water and so much green growth, there was an illusion of coolness. The trail led back and forth across the creek because of the ever-changing lay of the land, and Shannon, never abandoning those boot tracks, splashed through the water at each place where Murdock had done his fording.

He kept looking ahead as far down the canyon as he could see, but he failed to catch even a glimpse of the man he was tracking. He began to wonder if Murdock had had reason for coming into this gorge or if he were merely wandering aimlessly. So far he had seen no evidence that any other human, white or red, had traveled through it at any time. These mountains, this entire part of the desert, were unfamiliar to him. And how, he wondered, could Ben Murdock know where this seemingly endless gorge would take him? Was it possible that the black man possessed a homing instinct?

At midmorning Shannon came upon the ashes of a campfire. They were still warm to his touch, telling him that Murdock had stopped here within the past hour or two. Scattered about were the gnawed bones of some small animal. Looking around, Shannon found where the man had skinned and cleaned a rabbit he'd snared or shot.

I should have known he'd find food.

But a single jackrabbit would barely ease the hunger pangs of a man of Ben Murdock's size. He wouldn't keep his strength up with such fare. So Shannon told himself, but a part of him remained skeptical. Like him, Murdock would always survive on what little nature offered in this harsh land. The desert could provide sustenance if a man was not too picky about what he ate.

He stopped to rest at midday, choosing a place where the creek widened and formed a little pool. A cypress tree cast a dappled reflection over the water, and he could see his reflection on the surface as he bent to drink with his hat laid aside. His face was covered with wiry stubble and streaked with the grime of mingled dust and sweat. Naturally thin, it had grown gaunt and haggard. Deep lines were etched at the corners of his mouth, and his eyes were bloodshot. The manhunt was taking a toll of him, marking him.

Hombre, you look like hell.

He drank deeply, then splashed water against his face and scrubbed at the grime with his hands. He ducked his head into the pool, afterwards squeezing the water from his shaggy hair.

He ate some jerky, had a smoke, and pressed on. The canyon narrowed again, its walls pressing toward each other until they were but a few yards apart. Here were sheer cliffs instead of slopes. He thought he must be approaching the end of the gorge, but it widened again. It extended on and on through the mountain range. The vastness of it made Shannon feel puny indeed, and of little consequence in the overall scheme of things. He wondered if Murdock also felt as nothing here in the awesome enormity of the mountains.

At midafternoon he spotted the black man.

Although he had been hoping and even expecting

to see Murdock at any moment, Shannon was taken by surprise—was actually startled—upon catching a glimpse of him far ahead. He had only that: a mere glimpse. The next instant Murdock disappeared beyond some rocks. Lengthening and quickening his stride, Shannon sought to cut down the murderer's lead. He saw him again minutes later. Saw him, and lost him once more. They continued down the canyon in this manner, the hunter unable to overtake the hunted and the hunted failing to lose the hunter. They might have been playing a grim game of hide and seek.

The distance between them was perhaps a quarter of a mile, and it remained that for several hours. At one point, where the canyon floor was comparatively clear of brush and rocks, Shannon had his man within sight for many minutes. Then the gorge narrowed again, and Murdock vanished beyond a jutting elbow of the north wall. Making his way past this place fifteen minutes later, Shannon saw that the canyon did indeed have an ending; but it did not end as it had begun. Here was no gap in the mountains. Instead of an opening into the foothills, the canyon was sealed in by its walls coming together. A box canyon, with Murdock trapped in it.

The black man did not accept it as a trap, however. He was trying to climb from the gorge, making his difficult way over a massive pile of talus at the base of the cliff. Once he surmounted his pile of broken rock, which extended upward for at least a hundred feet, he would have a fair chance of escaping from the canyon. The talus had come from the crumbling away of the upper part of the cliff, and the broken area above offered a precarious but not impossible footing for a determined man.

Murdock was in trouble on the talus, however. Some of the broken rock must have fallen only recently and had not yet become firmly settled. It kept shifting under his weight, spilling away beneath his feet and hurtling downward in sizable rockslides. Burdened with his rifle and canteen, the black man could use but one hand to assist himself in his perilous ascent. He had difficulty keeping his footing and balance. But suddenly, as Shannon watched while running toward the base of the cliff, Murdock made a desperate scrambling effort that gained him the very top of the pile of talus. Another minute and he would be on firmer footing.

Shannon had no intention of giving him another minute. He stopped running, raised his rifle, and began driving slugs at the wall at a point just above Murdock's head. The wall consisted of shalelike rock that shattered under the impact of the slugs. At first only a few small fragments showered down on the climbing man, but then, with Shannon's seventh shot, a massive crumbling occurred. The weight and force of this fall knocked Murdock completely off balance. He went tumbling downward. The entire pile of talus, all those tons of broken rock, seemed to shift and slide. A cloud of dun-colored dust rose, obscuring everything and hiding Murdock from Shannon's sight.

Shannon ran forward again, gripped by a wild excitement and the certainty that he had his man. Then, from within the dust cloud, the buffalo gun boomed. Hearing the shriek of the heavy slug, Shannon dropped to the ground and crawled into a brush-fringed hollow that offered some cover. The Sharps fired again, and this time the slug came so close it kicked dirt into Shannon's face. He raised his head to look for Murdock, and a third shot whipped past within inches of him. He ducked down, making himself small in the hollow. He had failed to see the black man.

No more shots came, and he shouted, "Call it quits, Murdock! You're boxed in. This is the end of the trail for you!"

No reply came. None was necessary, Shannon realized. Murdock was well hidden and yet could bead Shannon's position here in the hollow. The black man couldn't get out of the canyon unless he were able to shoot his way out, and he was still reluctant to kill the man who wanted to take him in to be hanged. This was another standoff. They could only try to outwait each other. Murdock would sit tight until darkness came, Shannon knew. Then the murderer would try to slip past him. Suddenly, jokingly, Shannon realized that Murdock's unwillingness to kill him might not include a reluctance to cripple him.

He'll Injun up and jump me! Murdock, with his cat's eyes, rushing out of the darkness and swinging his buffalo gun like a club. He, Shannon, struck down and, when helpless, being disarmed. Murdock walking away from him laughing, maybe never to be found again. Shannon finally accepted the disquieting truth: he was matching wits with no ordinary man. Another upsetting truth might be that Ben Murdock was an abler man than Will Shannon.

How to outwit the black man?

Shannon felt that he had this choice: he could, with nightfall, either go in after Murdock and try to overpower him; or he could move from the hollow to another position and jump the man when he sought to leave his hiding place. The first plan seemed too risky; because of Murdock's ability to see in the dark he could not be surprised while in hiding. The latter plan, then. . . . With the coming of darkness Shannon gathered up his gear and crept out of the hollow.

A hundred yards down the canyon he came to some piled boulders that rose higher than his head by several feet. He left his saddlebags, war bag, and blanket at the base of the rocks and climbed with only his rifle. He lay prone on the highest rock, facing the canyon's box end. He had come to a decision. He must cripple the black man. He must shoot him through the right arm or shoulder to keep him from using his buffalo gun. It was that or shoot the man dead. And he could not, he admitted, kill a man who would kill him only as a last resort.

Take him in to be hanged, yes.

But kill him from ambush. . . . Shannon shook his head. That he couldn't do. He hadn't it in him to bushwhack even a murderer. Even crippling a man in such a manner would go against the grain. But Shannon had no choice . . .

CHAPTER SEVEN

Shannon woke with a start, alarm knifing through him. The strip of sky to be seen above the canyon walls was beginning to lighten with dawn. He had fallen asleep in spite of his having willed himself not to do so. He'd been dead to the world for . . . for how long?

Not for long, maybe. He had struggled against weariness during most of the night; he had fought drowsiness and lost the fight. All those long hours he had remained watchful, peering into the thick darkness for Murdock to make his try at escaping from the canyon's box end. And then, with the night nearly gone, he had slept.

He gazed toward the end of the canyon but could see nothing. The darkness was too deep. But he didn't need to see. He sensed that he was alone in the gorge.

He climbed down from the boulders. His sense of aloneness intensified, and a sort of panic swept through him.

"Murdock!" he shouted. "You there, black man?"

The only reply was an echo of his own voice, flung back at him by the canyon walls.

"Murdock, sing out! Give me an answer, damn you!"

To his own ears he sounded like a crazy man. It was crazy, his calling out to someone who was no longer within sound of his voice. He yelled no more, but he did curse bitterly under his breath. He cursed himself for having slept.

He returned to the boulders, planning to eat a meal before setting out to track the murderer all over again. He actually reached for his saddle-bags before becoming aware that they were not where he had left them. His war bag and blanket were there, but the saddlebags were gone. Murdock had taken them while he slept. Now the black man would eat well, while he must live off the land as best he could. Again, for all the good that it did him, Shannon cursed himself for having slept.

For breakfast, a drink of water and a cigarette. And a tightening of his belt. Two hours later finding where Murdock had left the canyon.

The black man had climbed the north wall, where it was a brush and saguaro-grown slope instead of a sheer rock cliff. The ascent was difficult, the slope being steeper than it appeared. Shannon was half an hour reaching the rim of the canyon. Here, beside the ashes of a fire, he found his saddlebags. They were considerably lighter because of the meal Murdock had fixed for himself. He had been considerate enough to dump the grounds from the coffee pot and wipe the grease from the frying pan. And, as though to taunt Shannon, he'd left a supply of firewood there.

Damn you, black man; if you're trying to get my goat, you've done it!

Shannon passed up the gift of the firewood. With the murderer having gained a long lead, he felt that he couldn't afford the time cooking a meal would require. He chewed on jerky as he set out after the man once more.

Again the tracks led west, deeper into the mountains.

Shannon had the thought that Murdock had left the saddlebags behind for a reason other than concern for him. The man evidently knew that one meal would see him through to where he could obtain another. Therefore he was not wandering aimlessly through these mountain heights. Somewhere beyond, Shannon was convinced, lay a ranch or a town at which Murdock expected to come by more food.

Outwit the black man?

Shannon shook his head, admitting there was little likelihood that he would get the better of Ben Murdock by matching wits with him. Or by trying to get the jump on him. He would have to find the man's weakness. And, damn it, he was sure to have one. The man didn't exist who didn't have a blind spot somewhere.

At midafternoon, with mountain slopes still all around him, Shannon was forced to stop and cook a meal. He had eaten the last of the jerky, and hunger was gnawing at his insides. He kindled a fire and brewed the last of his coffee. He fried what bacon he had left. He poured a batter of flour and water, with a pinch of salt added, into the hot bacon grease, making a pancake the size of the skillet and so thick it failed to cook in the middle. He ate with wolfish hunger and drained the coffee pot to the dregs.

He was so sure that Murdock was headed for some nearby inhabited place that he decided to lighten his burden. He left the pot and pan beside the dying fire. He dumped what flour, beans, and salt remained from the saddlebags and stowed in them his shaving gear and other things from his war bag. He also discarded his blanket. Starting out again, he had the saddlebags draped over his left shoulder, from which his canteen hung, and carried his rifle in his right hand. He struck out strongly, determined not to let Murdock continue to lengthen his lead.

He came out of the mountains late in the afternoon, having followed a ridge midway up a towering slope. He was above the line of desert growth, and the descent ahead of him was precipitous. He eyed the sheer slope with distrust. The tracks he followed showed that Murdock had descended safely by following a zigzagging course.

Looking out over the foothills below, Shannon

saw only an immensity of flat, rugged land. No ranch buildings or town lay in any direction. Seemingly, there had been no method to the madness that had taken Ben Murdock into the mountains. The man had not known where he would get his next meal. Shannon carefully scanned the hills and the desert beyond but saw nothing of the murderer. For a brief moment he had the eerie feeling that he was alone in the world. Stranger still, he felt that he had been abandoned by the black man. He grinned thinly, sourly amused at himself.

He started the treacherous descent, quartering downward as Murdock had done. He went slowly, with infinite care, always seeking the firmest footing. He was halfway down when the gravelly soil shifted beneath him. He lost his balance and hurtled downward, his tumbling weight starting a sizable landslide. He plunged a full fifty feet before coming to an abrupt, jolting stop against the fallen skeleton of a dead saguaro. He lay stunned for a long moment, wracked by pain and half buried by dirt.

He had clung to his rifle, saddlebags, and canteen, and finally he struggled to his feet. Knife-sharp pain shot through his left leg. When he tried to walk, the pain became so intense that he shifted his weight too quickly off that leg. He lost his balance and went sprawling again. He tumbled downward only a short distance this time, but he lost his gear. Slowly, agonizingly, he dragged himself upward to retrieve the rifle, saddlebags, and canteen. Pulling them after him, he tried crawling down the slope, but after a few minutes he had to give up the attempt. He was bathed with sweat and shaky all through. His leg throbbed steadily with pain, and he now had to accept the possibility that it was broken.

He pulled his pants leg up and with his pocket-knife cut away the leg of his drawers. The knee was swollen to half again its normal size. He probed it gingerly with anxious fingers but could not determine if there was a broken bone. He wet the piece of cotton underwear he'd cut away with water from the canteen and wrapped it about the knee. This helped not at all, for the dry air stole the moisture within minutes. He threw the cloth aside, pulled his pants leg down, and got out makings for a cigarette.

He considered his chances while he smoked, finding that he had none at all unless he were able to bear the terrible pain of placing his weight on the injured leg. He had already tested himself and been thrown flat for the effort. He was in a hell of a fix.

His cigarette smoked, he clenched his teeth against the pain and dragged himself up the slope again. After what seemed hours of torture, he reached the dead saguaro and with his knife hacked a slender five-foot-long piece of the fibrous wood from the skeleton. Hoping this stick would serve him as a makeshift crutch, he struggled erect and attempted to walk while leaning on it. The pain was still torment, but he forced himself to absorb it. He had covered half the distance to where his gear lay when the stick broke and he fell for a third time.

He lay for a while where he had landed, feeling defeated. Then, shrugging off despair, he inched downward on his stomach to his belongings. After he had drunk from the canteen, he lay back with his hat tipped over his eyes. He would rest awhile, then try again to get down off the slope.

He lay there until the sun went down, when, no longer burdened by its heat, he made a new attempt. His leg still wouldn't take his weight. He sank to the ground, after testing the injured knee, and with a sense of frustration, if not of defeat, began a crawling descent. He moved a few feet, pulled his gear after him, and repeated this maneuver. By nightfall he was only twenty yards closer to the base of the slope.

He continued his effort on into the night, moving a few feet at a time and suffering torment all the while. He came to realize the futility of what he was attempting. Even when and if he got off the slope, he would not have saved himself. Several miles of foothills lay beyond, and farther on there was only empty desert. He was done for, a goner. He accepted this hard fact fatalistically.

He would not lie helpless and die a lingering death. He would take the quick way out: put a bullet through his brain. Fear death? No, he had no such fear. He was more or less a godless man, but he was at peace with himself. He could face the hereafter, if any, for he had nothing of any consequence on his conscience.

He did have regrets. He was troubled because the black man had gotten away. And he realized that he had never really lived. His life as a soldier, a lawman, and a rancher had been rather meaningless. He had never known the contentment that Phil and Kate had achieved for a brief time. Compared to Sam and Lily Harbold, he had accomplished nothing. His life had been so empty that there was not even a single soul to mourn or miss him.

With the coming of the new day he found the instinct for self-preservation revived in him. He still could not stand, let alone walk, but once more he began crawling down the slope. At midmorning he was overcome by exhaustion. Again he lay flat on his back with his hat covering his eyes. He dozed off but woke with a start when a voice, real or dreamed, taunted him.

"What's wrong, ofay? You about to give up the ghost?"

Shannon removed his hat and propped himself up on his elbows, wincing with pain at even this slight movement. He hadn't dreamed the voice.

Murdock had spoken. He was squatting there, bracing himself on the sharp incline with his Sharps rifle. He was grinning hugely, with a glint of that gold tooth. His scar puckered hideously with the grin.

"Saw you take your fall yesterday afternoon, boss," he said. "Been watching you this morning, from down in the hills where there's a nice, cool spring. Killed a deer yesterday before you got this far. Me, I've been eating good. What ails you, a busted leg?"

"Busted or sprained," Shannon said. "I don't know which. Not that it matters. One or the other, it's got me laid low."

"Want me to take a look?"

"You're a doctor too, are you?"

"I've patched some wounds and set some bones in my time."

Murdock laid his rifle down, well beyond Shannon's reach. Shannon realized tardily that his own rifle and also his revolver were missing. The black man had taken them before waking him. They lay some distance up the slope, where he had thrown them.

"I'm not asking any favors of you, Murdock."

"Shucks, boss; I'd do as much for a stray dog."

He worked Shannon's pants leg up over the injured knee, which was enormously swollen and fiery red. With the thick-knuckled fingers of his big hands, he felt gently of the knee. He grasped the ankle and slowly forced the knee to bend. The pain was sheer agony for Shannon. He clenched his teeth and managed to not even whimper.

"Twisted," Murdock said, working the pants leg down. "A bad sprain. You'll be over it in a few days, with care."

"In a few days I'll be dead of thirst or heat-stroke."

"Not if I can help it," Murdock said. "Put on your hat and pick up your saddlebags and canteen."

"What for?"

"For me to get you down from here."

"I told you I don't want any favors from you."

"Could be that you'll be doing me one."

"How do you figure that, you loco black bastard?"

"Well, I'll tell you, boss," Murdock said. "Back when I got old enough to savvy what the world was like, back when I was a sapling on that plantation, along with a couple of hundred other slaves, I set out to prove myself as good a man as any white-skinned hombre. I've proved it a hundred times, over the years. Now you, boss, you're a damn good man in my opinion. *Mucho hombre*, as the Mex say. If I get you down from here, when you can't do it yourself, I'll have proven that I'm a better man than you. So you'll be doing me a favor by letting me try it."

"You're loco, all right. You know that, Murdock?"

"If I'm loco, what are you, tracking me all this way when you hadn't a chance of taking me prisoner?"

"So we're both crazy men," Shannon said, putting on his hat and reaching for his saddlebags and canteen. "You do me a favor and I do you one. Help me up, damn it."

Murdock picked up his rifle, then helped Shannon rise and stand one-legged. With his left arm about the black man's broad shoulders, Shannon leaned heavily against him. Murdock took him about the middle with his right arm. They began moving slowly down the slope, Murdock finding secure footing for both of them. In an hour they were down off of the slope, both out of breath and sweating profusely. They sank to the ground, and Shannon began rubbing his bad knee.

"How much farther to this spring of yours?" he demanded.

"A good half a mile," Murdock told him. "You got any makings?"

Shannon got out and handed him his tobacco and papers. Murdock rolled a cigarette for each of them and then struck a match with his thumbnail.

After accepting a light, Shannon said, "I took it that you knew where you were headed. But you're lost. You're going around in circles." His tone was mocking. "Shucks, man; I expected better of you."

Murdock shook his head. "I'm never lost, boss. I'd never been through that canyon back yonder, but I figured it would have a box end. My idea was that I could get out before you caught up with me; and I could lose you for good. My mistake." He gestured toward the foothills. "There's a road yonder. If you didn't see it from up there, it's because it runs close to the base of the hills."

"So there's a road. But is there any traffic on it?"

"Sure. Stagecoaches and freight rigs. It runs from Lode City to Tucson."

"Let's get over to it, then."

"After I've fed you and doctored your knee," Murdock said. "Ain't no need for you to be in a hurry now." Again he grinned, this time mockingly. "You're safe with me, boss."

With Murdock again supporting Shannon, they made it to the spring an hour later. It was not far into the foothills, but they had been forced to take a roundabout route for the easiest possible going. The water trickled from the rocky cutbank of a dry wash and formed a little pool before draining off to be swallowed up by the arid soil.

Murdock had butchered out his deer some distance away and had cooked a haunch on a makeshift spit beside the pool. Now he cut off a large piece of the venison with the knife he carried sheathed on the belt of his gun rig. He handed the meat to Shannon, who had seated himself with his back to the cutbank. Shannon tore at it with his teeth wolfishly. Half-starved, he imagined that the venison tasted better than anything he'd ever eaten.

"You'd get mighty sick of that after a day or two," Murdock said, watching him amusedly. "Without salt and side dishes, meat don't go so good for long."

"I'm not complaining, am I?" Shannon said, his mouth full.

"Didn't say that you were. Just keep on filling your belly while I have another look at your knee."

He rummaged in the saddlebags and found what he sought: Shannon's spare shirt. He soaked the shirt at the spring, then wrapped it about the swollen knee.

"Keep it wet," he said. "That spring water is cold, and it'll take the swelling down." Picking up his rifle, he added, "I'll be back by and by."

"I won't be counting on it," Shannon said. "Thanks for bringing me down here. But don't get the idea that I won't be coming after you, once I'm back on my feet. Your saving my life doesn't change anything."

"I'll be back, I tell you."

"Why?"

"That leg won't carry you far for a long time,"

Murdock told him. "You need a horse, ofay."

"And you're getting one for me, are you?"

"That's why I'm heading out."

"Just where do you figure you'll find one, here in the middle of nowhere?"

His voice edged with sarcasm, Murdock said, "A white man with his superior brain ought to be able to figure it out if a black man can with his inferior brain."

Anger hardening his whiskery face, Shannon said, "Listen, you; I never said a word about being superior to you."

"You think it, though, don't you?"

"You don't know what's in my mind, black man. You know what your trouble is?"

"What is my trouble, boss? Other than having been born black?"

"You let it stick in your craw that you're black and keep thinking of yourself as a 'nigger' when nobody's calling you one."

"I've been called 'nigger' a million times, ofay."

"Well, I'll tell you something," Shannon said. "You're the first man who ever called me 'ofay.' It must be as bad a word as 'nigger,' or you wouldn't be tagging me with it. You know damn well why I've got it in for you. It's not because you're black but because you murdered a woman."

Murdock flinched visibly. He said, "Our

calling each other names ain't doing either of us any good. This stage road yonder . . . stagelines always have way stations every twenty or twenty-five miles. I was out there and had a look. There's no station in either direction for as far as I could see. So I'll have a long hike ahead of me; but it shouldn't be, the way I figure, much more than ten miles, and maybe less than that."

"All right," Shannon said grudgingly. "Now I savvy. And I should have figured it out for myself. How are you planning to get a horse at the stage station? With that buffalo gun of yours?"

"Not one horse—two," Murdock said. "You don't think I'm going to keep on hoofing it, do you? Sure, I'll use my buffalo gun if the agent won't sell the broncs." Defiantly, he added, "I've got some money. And it was come by honest."

"No agent will sell you company horses, and you know it."

"All the same, I'll be coming back with a couple."

"So you're a horse thief along with everything else."

"Maybe I won't need to be that, with your badge."

Looking at him uncertainly, Shannon said, "What are you talking about?" Then he remembered the deputy sheriff's badge pinned to his shirt front. "You really think anybody would take you for a lawman, a black man like you?"

"You figure anybody'd call me a liar after taking a good, hard look at me?"

Shannon took a good, hard look at him. All these days of having been on the run hadn't marked the black man. He hadn't become gaunted. He showed no signs of weariness. He didn't even look dirty. That instant Shannon realized that Murdock had washed his clothes upon finding this spring. He'd shaved too, probably with the knife on his belt. But for the scar he looked fine. Because of the scar, along with his great size, it wasn't likely that the agent of an isolated stage station would tell him to his face that he couldn't be a lawman because of his black hide.

"Nothing doing," Shannon said. "You're not using this badge to palm yourself off as a peace officer."

"I'm doing this partly for you, damn it."

"Quit doing me favors, now that we're even Stephen."

"Shannon, I'm having that badge," Murdock said, coming closer to where Shannon was seated. "One way or another."

"Try and take it," Shannon said. "Game leg or no, I'll give you a fight if you do. And you know mighty well that it's still not proven that you're a better man than I am."

"If I fight you, one of us will end up dead.

And it's not right for friends to kill each other."

"Friends? Why, you loco black—"

Murdock swung his buffalo gun like a club. The blow was aimed at Shannon's hurt knee, and it landed solidly. Pain exploded all through him, paralyzing and blinding him. He fell onto his side, hearing himself moan and sensing that Murdock was removing the nickel-plated star from his shirt. He tried to curse the black man, but something was wrong with his vocal cords. He could utter only croaking noises. After a long moment, when the awful pain subsided, he forced himself back to his sitting position and saw that Murdock was already a hundred yards off and moving at a dogtrot on his way through the hills.

Recovering his power of speech, Shannon swore bitterly. His mind was full of dark thoughts of revenge. Finally he hauled himself up short mentally, telling himself that this was probably the last he would see of the black man, until he hunted him down again.

He'll get a horse at the stage station—just one horse—and head for parts unknown.

And yet, during the hours that followed, Shannon kept watching for Murdock's return. He was unable to convince himself that the black man was a liar. A murderer, yes. But not a liar.

Three hours after he'd walked away from the spring, Murdock returned on horseback. The animal he rode was a sorry-looking nag of the sort a rancher would have called "crowbait" and spurned. A chestnut with bald spots, it was scrawny and short winded. It breathed wheezily as Murdock reined it in, its sides heaving. He had no second mount in tow.

"So the station agent decided you were half lawman and half liar," Shannon said. "Because of that he let you have only one horse, if you call that a horse. Am I right?"

Murdock wore the six-pointed star on his shirt. He'd given it a polishing, and the nickel gave off a silvery sheen in the sunlight.

"Not altogether right," he said. "This was the only bronc in his stable that was saddle broke. Besides, he had only one saddle. Look, Shannon; I'm going after your rifle and six-shooter. It could be we'll need all the guns we can get hold of."

"Why? What's up?"

"No stagecoaches are running because of the Indian scare. Orders from the company office at Tucson. There was one from Lode City this morning and it's lying over at the Lost Squaw Gulch station, where I got this nag. That's about eight, nine miles north of here. Some Apaches passed there late yesterday and fired a few shots at the buildings. So we'd both better be armed."

"That's only sensible," Shannon said.

Murdock swung his sorry mount closer, took a bottle from inside his shirt, and handed it down to Shannon.

"Horse liniment," he said. "Good for man or beast. The agent gave it to me when I told him I had a prisoner out here with a game leg."

"A prisoner! Damn it, Murdock—"

"Rub it on your knee while I'm gone," Murdock said, and rode off laughing.

The knee's swelling had gone down considerably, and its pain was less severe. Shannon applied the liniment, which touched off a burning sensation on the skin and seemed to penetrate to the joint with its warmth. He tried standing, slowly placing his weight on the injured leg. The pain returned, again knife sharp, but he persisted and was still on his feet, leaning against the cutbank, when Murdock returned.

The black man dismounted from the borrowed horse, laid both rifles—his own and Shannon's—and the latter's revolver on the ground, then led the animal close to Shannon.

"Mount up," he said. "I'll give you a boost."

Shannon hopped one-legged to the chestnut, took hold of his mane and the reins with his left hand, and grasped the saddle horn with his right. Ever so slowly, he raised his left foot to the stirrup. There was tearing pain, and he felt himself break out in a sweat. Murdock gripped him by the hips, making ready to lift him.

"Say the word when you're ready, ofay."

"Wait," Shannon said. "Give me a second . . ."

He lowered his leg, gave up his hold on the

horse, and swung around as Murdock let go of him.

He grabbed for the black man's revolver, jerked it from its holster, and swung it high. Taken completely by surprise, Murdock reacted laggardly. He tried to get hold of the gun, then he sought to block the blow with his arm. He failed to do either. Shannon struck with all his might, and the barrel of the gun caught Murdock over the left temple. The clubbing blow drove the black man to his hands and knees.

Shannon struck again, this time to the base of the skull, and knocked him flat. He threw the gun away and straddled the fallen man in a kneeling position that brought on the expected almost unbearable pain. He pulled the handcuffs from his hip pocket, removed the key from one of the locks, and pocketed it. He grasped Murdock's left arm and snapped one of the cuffs on its wrist. He was reaching for the man's right arm when Murdock gave a violent heave and sent Shannon toppling from his back.

Shannon fell onto his left side, wrenching the injured knee again. Murdock flung himself upon him and took him by the throat. The scarred black face was contorted with rage and hatred. His throttling grip tightened, cutting off Shannon's breathing. Shannon grabbed the thick black wrists, but he hadn't the strength to break the viselike hold of Murdock's hands. His lungs felt about to burst, and his vision blurred. Panic came to him, and he flailed at the black man with weakening arms. He had the frightening thought that this was the end for him.

CHAPTER EIGHT

By chance Shannon's right hand fell upon the hilt of the knife on Murdock's belt. Acting more by instinct than by thought, for his mind was reeling, he drew the knife from its sheath and struck at the black man with it. He lacked the strength to drive it all the way home, but the point pierced shirt and skin. And Murdock, reacting to a greater danger than actually threatened him, broke his hold on Shannon's throat and flung himself away from the bloodied blade.

Shannon was too weakened and pain wracked to follow up his advantage. He dropped the knife and put his hands to his throat as he gasped for air. Nausea assailed him, and he turned onto his side and went through a dry retching. When his stomach stopped its heaving, he forced himself to a sitting position and saw blurredly that Murdock had retrieved his revolver and knife. The man stood ten feet away with the gun cocked and aimed.

"Shannon, I ought to do for you!"

"Go ahead," he said hoarsely. "I can't stop you."

"You're an ungrateful bastard!"

"Maybe I am," Shannon said. "I'll sure keep trying to get you to the gallows as long as I can draw breath."

“I’m leaving you here,” Murdock said. “I don’t owe you anything anymore. Hand over the key to these handcuffs.”

Shannon gave him the key, and the black man removed the manacles from his left wrist. He put them and the key away in his pocket. Blood trickled down the scarred side of his face from a gash opened by the blow of the gun barrel. His shirt was stained red at the left side where the knife had cut him. He stared at Shannon with hatred for a moment longer, then he holstered his gun and went to the pool.

Removing his hat and shirt, he washed his wounds. His upper body was heavily corded with muscles. Across his broad back was a ladder of welts that had certainly been put there by an overseer’s whip. Evidently he had not been a wholly docile slave. He picked up the bottle of liniment and applied some of the fiery liquid to the gash at his temple and the cut at his side. Returning to the pool, he washed the blood from his shirt. His fastidiousness made Shannon uncomfortably aware of his own grubby appearance. He had the thought that Murdock did look the part of a lawman and he that of a fugitive. Murdock pulled his wet shirt on, donned his hat, and came to where Shannon sat.

“On your feet,” he ordered. “We’ll try it again.”

Shannon started to protest again that he wanted no favors done him but thought better of it.

Anything he might say at the moment would have the false ring of a counterfeit coin. He retrieved his hat, which he had lost during the struggle, and forced himself erect. He limped to the crowbait horse. With a boost from Murdock, he gained the saddle with a minimum of pain. Murdock picked up the saddlebags and put the liniment, the shirt, and the revolver into them. He picked up the two rifles.

Giving Shannon a sour look, he said, "Move out."

Shannon kneed the horse into motion and headed through the hills. The chestnut had a sluggish gait, and Murdock, coming along behind, had no difficulty in keeping up. Emerging from the hills, they turned north along the road running past their base. Murdock strode along in a sullen silence, and Shannon was lost in gloom.

Late in the afternoon they topped a rise and saw the stage station ahead. It was located midway through a gap in the hills. A long grade led down to it, for the gap was actually a steep-walled gulch. The adobe buildings, a house and a stable, were located at the west side, close to the wall there. They stood at the widest part of the gulch, which was about two hundred yards across. The cliffs rose to a height of about eighty feet, and the one to the west had an overhanging shelf of rock midway up that jutted out over the station like a canopy.

"Pull up," Murdock said, again making it an order.

Shannon obeyed. Caught off guard, he found the black man slipping the handcuffs onto his wrists before he could even protest, let alone resist. Murdock grinned at him with mingled amusement and malice.

"That's to convince the folks up ahead that you are my prisoner . . . and a real bad hombre," he said. "I can't have you making out to them that you're something else." Shannon stared at his manacled wrists with helpless anger, then looked at the black man. "You never miss a trick, do you, Murdock?"

"Not me. Not when my neck is in danger of getting stretched."

"You figuring on staying here for a while?"

"Only long enough to look over those company horses for one likely to carry me far and fast. I aim to pick out the best of the bunch and ride it out, saddle broke or not."

"Don't expect me to wish you luck."

Murdock laughed, seemingly in high spirits again. Always mercurial of mood, he was rid of the anger and hatred that Shannon's gun whipping of him had brought on. Shannon's own feelings fluctuated to lesser degree. He remained in a low mood, bitter because the black man managed to get the better of him at every turn. He was far from ready to admit that Ben Murdock was the better man, but he did resent his ability to win every hand dealt him.

He rode on toward the station, the chestnut horse now quickening its pace as it descended into the gulch. Aware that it was almost home, the animal was eager to arrive there. Murdock came to walk beside the horse, having retrieved the rifles and saddlebags from where he'd laid them to handcuff Shannon.

"You ain't got much to say anymore, ofay. The cat got your tongue?"

Shannon gave him a scowling look. "I've been doing a lot of wondering about you, black man. You've got to have a weak spot, and I've been trying to figure out what it is."

Again Murdock laughed, the sound rolling out of him rich and hearty. "I've got one. A real big one. It's there for you to see, and has been since the first time we ran into each other. I'm not telling you what it is, though. Why should I, when you don't take to my doing you favors?"

Shannon stared at him blankly, having not the slightest idea what he was talking about.

When they entered the gulch, Shannon had the sensation of being hemmed in, trapped. Considering that this had always been Apache country, he thought it strange indeed that a stage station had been located between high rock walls. He found it stranger still that the place had never been burned to the ground by Geronimo,

Delgado, or some other warring Apache chieftain.

He said, "This is sure no place to hole up in with Delgado on the loose."

"I'm not worrying about it," Murdock said. "I'll be moving on before sunup tomorrow."

The adobe wall that enclosed the buildings, a corral, and a sizable yard was five feet high and thick enough to stop bullets. If there had ever been a gate, nothing of it remained. The opening in the front wall was wide enough to permit the passage of a stagecoach, or a whole swarm of Apache warriors. The stagecoach that was lying over until Delgado was rounded up stood beside the barn, its traces empty. A dozen or more horses were in the corral. The water supply was a well located midway between the station house and the stable. Its circular stone wall rose to a height of three feet and had two wooden posts that supported a roof. Buckets of water could be drawn by means of a windlass.

Three men lounged beneath the wooden awning that ran across the front of the house. Two were seated on a bench, and the third leaned against a post. Nothing in their lax attitude suggested that they were fearful of an Apache attack. Only one person kept watch at the gateway. This was a boy of seven or eight who was armed with a handgun whittled out of wood. He raised the make-believe gun and aimed it at Shannon.

"You a bad man, mister?" he demanded. Without waiting for an answer, he added, "If you are, you'd better stick 'em up . . . pronto!"

Shannon took him to be one of the stagecoach passengers. He was wearing his Sunday best: a white shirt with a string tie, gray knee pants, black stockings and shoes, and a visored cap. Tufts of yellow hair stuck out from beneath the cap, and his small face, an impish face, was pug-nosed and heavily freckled. His ears stuck out from his head like the handles of a china bowl. As Shannon reined in, the boy lost his bravado and stared at him with mingled awe and fright. His mouth fell open, revealing gaps at either side of his two big, new front teeth. A vagrant thought came to Shannon: *this was me a quarter of a century ago.* He too had been a smart-alecky but easily spooked kid.

Raising his manacled hands, he said, "Don't shoot, mister. I'm not as bad as I look."

"Aw, shucks; this ain't a real gun."

"It looks pretty real to me. You a lawman?"

"Aw, you're funning me."

"Sure, I am, son."

Over being frightened by Shannon's tough, grubby appearance, the boy said, "You sure look bad . . . and mean. What'd you do, anyway? Rob a bank? Hold up a train?"

Before Shannon could think of how to answer that a woman's voice called out in high alarm.

"Tommy, come away from there! Tommy Edwards, do you hear me? Come here this instant!"

"That your ma calling, son?"

"Yeah."

"You'd better do as she wants."

"Aw, she won't let me do nothing ever."

The woman called out again, and Shannon looked in her direction just as she stepped from the doorway of the house and started across the yard. He looked with mere curiosity, then stared with abrupt interest. She was an extremely attractive young woman despite her look of exasperation over the boy's disobedience. She was tall and sturdy, blond of hair, and fair of complexion. Surprisingly, her eyes were a dark brown. She wore a becoming pale green shirtwaist and a skirt of a deeper green. She was such a woman as to make a man very much aware of his maleness, and Shannon, to his chagrin, experienced a triggering of desire.

The boy tried to dodge away from her, but she caught him deftly by the seat of his britches.

"When I speak to you, young man, I expect you to listen," she told him, transferring her grip to one of his flaring ears. "Now march yourself around back of the house for a paddling. March, I say!"

Tommy howled as though he were already being flayed to within an inch of his young life.

"Ma, don't! Let go of me, Ma! You're tearing my ear off, honest!"

Shannon said, "Ma'am, it could be that you are hurting the boy."

Her angry gaze whipped around to him. "I'll thank you to keep out of this. I'll chastise my child as much as necessary to keep him from associating with the likes of you!"

With that she led the boy away.

Stung to the quick, Shannon looked after them with an anger of his own. It flared into rage as Murdock's mocking laughter rang out.

"The lady sure thinks you're a real lawbreaker, ofay," the black man said. Then, prodding him in the back with one of the rifles, he ordered, "Move on, prisoner. Head for the stable. It ain't likely that those folks over at the house want you associating with them."

Murdock laughed again as though enjoying the situation immensely.

CHAPTER NINE

Stared at by the three men over by the station house, Shannon rode the now played-out chestnut horse across the yard and reined it in by the stable. Murdock helped him dismount out of regard for the restraining handcuffs and his injured knee. A youth of about eighteen came from the building and gazed at Shannon with childish wonder. His dull-witted but pleasant face broke into a sudden bucktoothed smile that his guileless china blue eyes seemed to reflect.

Taking the horse's reins, the youth said, "I'm Benjy. What's your name, mister?"

Shannon realized that here was one of those backward souls who did not need to be regarded as unfortunate because of their retarded condition. In spite of, or perhaps because of, their laggard mental faculties, they were by nature habitually cheerful.

"My name's Will Shannon, Benjy. Thanks for the loan of the horse."

"Oh, Ginger ain't mine," Benjy said. "He's Mr. Harper's. Mr. Harper is my boss. But I take care of Ginger, like I do the company horses. I'm mighty glad to see you, Mr. Shannon. Folks don't often stop here, except for the little time while the stages change teams, but now we've got a whole passel of visitors. Two of them are nice ladies. You an outlaw, Mr. Shannon?"

"So this black man would have you believe."

"That's funny, ain't it. A nigger sheriff?"

"Don't call him nigger, Benjy. He doesn't like it."

"If you're an outlaw, maybe you know Jesse James?"

"No, I can't say that I do."

"That's too bad," Benjy said. "Well, I've got to take care of old Ginger. I'll talk to you some more, Mr. Shannon."

"You do that, Benjy."

As the youth started toward the corral with the chestnut, Murdock said, "Make yourself at home, Shannon. I'm going over to the house and put these shooting irons where they'll be out of your reach, you being such a desperate outlaw and all."

He strode to the house, entered it, and did not immediately reappear. Shannon seated himself on the ground with his back to the stable wall, sighing with relief to get his weight off his left leg. The boy and his mother came from behind the house. He was crying, and she wore a look of maternal severity. After giving him a final talking-to, she entered the house. He stopped crying the instant she was gone. Stealing a look at Shannon, he began to edge in his direction while kicking a small stick this way and that with feigned concentration. Finally he was within five yards of Shannon.

"Listen, son: if your mother doesn't want you talking to me, you'd better obey her."

"I ain't talking to you," Tommy said. "Besides. . . ." A sly grin came to his freckled face. "Besides, she won't wallop me hard. She only gave me five licks this time. Didn't hurt me none. Hurt her more than me, like she always says."

Shannon grinned back at him, thinking that here was a youngster after his own heart. "Still, you shouldn't get her all riled up."

Looking hurt, Tommy said, "You don't want to talk to me?"

"Sure, I do. But your ma—"

"She says you'd be a bad influence on a kid."

"Oh, I'm not all that much of a wrong one."

"You ever kill anybody?"

"Now, boy, none of that kind of talk," Shannon said. "If you've got to gab with me, gab about something else. What's your last name?"

"Edwards."

"Where do you live?"

"Nowhere."

"Nowhere? Quit pulling my leg, boy. Everybody's got to live someplace."

Tommy picked up the stick and tossed it into the air. It fell midway between himself and Shannon. He came to pick it up again and remained there.

"Them handcuffs," he said. "You can't bust out of them?"

"No, I can't," Shannon said. "Now where do you live? Lode City? Tucson?"

"We don't live noplace now. We used to live at Lode City, but my pa got killed."

"Your pa is dead? I'm sorry to hear that."

"He got killed in a mine accident. He was super'tendent of the Lucky Widow Mine that Mr. Mathison owns. That's Mr. Mathison over there, smoking the cigar. That big man with the red face. He's rich."

"When did it happen, the mine accident?"

"About a month ago, I guess."

Shannon saw Tommy's mother appear at the doorway. When she saw where the boy was, she came marching across the yard with that look of exasperation on her attractive face again. Tommy became aware of her approach and darted off toward the corral, calling out to Benjy. She stopped and stared after him, biting down on her lower lip in her frustration.

"Don't worry about him, ma'am," Shannon said. "He won't be influenced the wrong way by me. He was just telling me about his father . . . about the mine accident."

She looked at him frowningly, then she ventured closer. "I'd rather you wouldn't encourage him. He's so very hard to handle lately. He misses his father, even though he doesn't show it. I believe he is grieving inside and hides it by being naughty."

Struggling to his feet, Shannon removed his hat and looked at her sympathetically. "I'm sorry about your husband, Mrs. Edwards. Losing him must be hard on both of you, since it's been only a month."

"A month? Did Tommy tell you that? It's been more than three, actually. He has no sense of time, I'm afraid. But, yes, losing his father was hard on both of us."

Shannon imagined that he could see grief in her eyes now. And that for an instant she had a lost, lonely look.

He said, "Set your mind at rest about the youngster, Mrs. Edwards. I'll not say anything to him that he shouldn't hear."

She gazed at him intently, studying him, and he was again uncomfortably aware of his seedy appearance. He could see strength of character in her face, and he had the impression that she was bearing up well and would endure the stresses and strains of widowhood. But he thought it a shame that she had been widowed so young. She was only now fully blooming as a woman. Her expression softened, and she regarded him with what he thought was pity. He guessed at her thoughts: she believed him to be on his way to prison or even the gallows. For an instant he thought of telling her the truth, then he realized that she wouldn't believe it. In her place, he wouldn't have believed it.

She said, "Well, since you promise not to tell Tommy things a small boy shouldn't hear, Mr. . . ."

"Shannon, Mrs. Edwards. Will Shannon."

She nodded and said, "If he pesters you too much, just tell him to go away. I won't be offended if you're cross to him."

Shannon shook his head. "I won't be that to him. It could be that he needs to talk to a man, missing his father as he does."

"That could be so. But he doesn't make up with the . . ."

As she broke off, looking embarrassed, Shannon said, "With the right kind of men. Is that what you wanted to say, ma'am?"

She flushed, and the color suffusing her cheeks enhanced her attractiveness. She seemed to feel she should apologize but didn't know how.

"It's all right," he told her. "You've every reason to think me the wrong kind."

Ben Murdock appeared, for once not burdened by his buffalo gun. He was smoking a cigar and looking smugly satisfied with himself. He removed his hat, took the cigar from his mouth, and bowed to Mrs. Edwards.

"My prisoner hasn't been annoying you, has he, ma'am?" His voice was gentle, his tone respectful. He kept the scarred side of his face turned from her. “I hope he hasn’t spoken out of turn, ma’am.”

“Oh, no, not at all,” she said. “Those handcuffs seem so uncomfortable for him. Are they really necessary?”

Murdock made a show of considering that, looking at Shannon with an uncertain frown. “I suppose I could risk removing them, ma’am. He’s not a real bad hombre. I don’t think he’d do anybody harm.”

He put his hat back on his head, gripped the cigar between his teeth, and got out the key to the handcuffs.

Coming to Shannon, he said, “I’ll be keeping a close watch on you, mister.”

Shannon didn’t feel it necessary to reply to that.

When the handcuffs were removed, Mrs. Edwards said, “Is there anything I can get you, Mr. Shannon? A cup of coffee, maybe?”

“That’s real kind of you, ma’am. I could do with a cup.”

“I’ll bring it right away,” she said, and turned toward thc housc.

She had taken only two or three steps when the shot came. Shannon saw something kick up dirt just ahead of her and then heard the report of the rifle. He turned startled eyes toward the rim of the gulch’s east wall. An Apache was there. He had fired from a kneeling position and was now aiming for a second shot. Shannon moved, limping, toward the woman, who stood as though frozen by fright. Murdock caught her by the arm and swung her about as the Apache's rifle cracked a second time. He pushed her toward Shannon. Then he swung about and drew his long-barreled Colt's revolver. He began firing at the Apache. Shannon drew Mrs. Edwards toward the stable doorway. She tried to pull away from him.

"My boy . . . I must get my boy!"

Shannon said, "I'll get him," and pushed her into the stable. "Stay there. I mean that. Stay there!"

He broke into a hobbling run, hearing Murdock's six-shooter trading shots with the Apache's rifle. He rounded the corner of the building and saw Benjy holding Tommy on his shoulder so the boy could see over the corral wall and watch the horses. The pair seemed unaware of the gunfire.

"You, Benjy!" Shannon shouted. "Come here with the boy!"

The youth stared at him dull wittedly, not moving until Shannon reached them and grabbed him by the arm. He became frightened when Shannon pulled him away from the corral, out of harm's way, and took Tommy into his own arms. But it was not because of the shooting that he was scared.

"I didn't do anything wrong, Mr. Shannon. I was just showing Tommy the horses."

"Didn't you hear the shooting, for God's sake?"

Benjy shook his head, looking bewildered.

Tommy said, "I heard it, and I was scared." His eyes had grown round in his freckled face; their irises were, Shannon noticed, the same deep brown as his mother's. "Was somebody shooting at you, mister? Was it the sheriff?"

"An Indian was shooting at us, and the sheriff shot back at him. I'll take you to your mother. Benjy, you come with us. Stick close. You hear?"

"I hear you, Mr. Shannon."

Shannon carried the boy to the corner of the building and looked across the yard. Ben Murdock stood close to the house now. He'd been inside it and had gotten his Sharps rifle. He was gazing steadily up at the cliff top where the Apache had appeared. The three men who had been lounging in front of the house had vanished inside. Their place beneath the wooden awning had been taken by a burly, bearded man who also held a rifle and watched the opposite height.

Benjy said, "That's Mr. Harper. He'll fix that Injun, sure. He's my boss, Mr. Harper is."

"Come on," Shannon said. "This way . . . into the stable."

He went around the corner and along the front of the stable. Tommy's mother stood just inside the doorway. She took her son from Shannon and hugged him to her.

"Oh, thank heaven!"

Shannon said, "Stay here until we're sure there's no more danger. You will?"

Seeing her nod her head, he turned and went into the yard. The Apache was no longer in sight. He limped painfully to where Murdock stood.

"Did you nail him?"

"With a handgun?" the black man said. "Not likely."

"There's got to be more than that one."

"Not far off, anyway."

"He'll be back with them."

"Now that is likely," Murdock said. "And like you put it a while back, this is no place to hole up when the Apaches are on the warpath."

"I'm going after my guns," Shannon said. "You'll have to shoot me to stop me."

"I'll save my shooting for the redskins, ofay. Like you'd better do."

Shannon made his painful way to the house, and Benjy's boss, Mr. Harper, stared at him with the fear and distrust with which criminals were always viewed. A big man, the station agent, but his bulk was not brawn. He was soft and flabby, a man given to indulging but not exerting himself. He had a paunch that bulged hugely over his belt. His unkempt beard failed to hide sagging jowls. His nose was bulbous and a purplish red. His eyes were badly bloodshot. Shannon knew him for a boozer even before he caught the smell of rotgut whiskey on his breath.

“That jig deputy letting you run loose?” Harper said. He sounded disapproving.

“He’s going to need my guns,” Shannon said. “And you, friend, are going to need to be sober. You’d better give that jug of yours a rest until Delgado is rounded up.”

Harper’s expression curdled. “Now, hold on, you. I don’t take that kind of talk from no two-bit outlaw. Any more lip from you and, by damn, I’ll—”

“You’ll go on the wagon and stay on it,” Shannon cut in, using a rough tongue. “You’ve got people here to keep safe, a couple women and a kid among them. You sober up; and stay sober.”

He went into the house, ignoring the cussing-out the agent gave him to his back.

He found three men and a woman in the main room of the house. They were frozen in attitudes of frightened expectancy. Two of the men were at the windows, which looked out to the yard. Each of them was armed with a revolver. The third man stood in the center of the room facing the doorway. He held a rifle. The woman stood by the fireplace at the end of the room. A glance at her told Shannon that she was armed only with a tawdry sort of beauty. The four stared at him as Harper had done, with fear and distrust.

He looked around for his rifle and saddlebags. The latter lay in a corner of the room. He went to them and took out his revolver. Slipping the gun into his holster, he approached the man with the rifle.

"That happens to be mine, friend. I'll trouble you for it."

"Listen, I may need it to defend myself," the man said, his voice off key and shaky with nervousness, "if those red savages come down here. . . . Anyway, you've got a revolver."

A short and pudgy man, he was dapper in a brown plaid suit and a round hard hat. His full-moon face was pale and sweaty, telling of how great a fear that Apache's shots had touched off in him. A city man, Shannon thought; probably a drummer out from St. Louis or Kansas City. Just as probably, he didn't know how to use a rifle.

"If they come down here, those red savages," Shannon told him, "I'll be able to make better use of that Winchester than you. But let's not argue the point. Just hand it over."

One of the men at the windows said, "Just hold onto it, Shapely. I don't like the idea of this outlaw being turned loose and armed, anyway. That black deputy is playing the fool, letting him have the run of the place."

His gaunt, unshaven face turned rock hard, Shannon shifted his gaze to the speaker. This was the mine owner, Mr. Mathison: little Tommy Edwards's "rich man." Mathison was heavy bodied in a black broadcloth suit and a silk vest embroidered with a floral design. His pomaded hair was a steel gray, as was the neatly cropped mustache that adorned his square, ruddy face. He had the arrogant manner that was part and parcel of most moneyed men. In his case, at this moment, that arrogance was near belligerence. He gave the impression, to Shannon at least, that he was a dangerous man to cross.

Rubbed the wrong way by him, Shannon didn't care whether he was dangerous or not. He said, "That's bad advice you gave your friend, Mathison. Because of it, I take it that you're one of those hombres who stand back and yell 'let's you and him fight.' "

Mathison was stung. His heavy face became an even deeper shade of red, and he shot an anxious glance at the woman as though fearing he was being made to look small in her eyes. Then he scowled at Shannon, took a step in his direction, and raised his gun threateningly. It was a short-barreled revolver, probably of thirty-two-caliber. A gentleman's gun.

"Get out of here," he said in flat command. "You're not fit to mix with decent people. Go on, move!"

This, Shannon thought, was what came of Murdock's making him out a criminal. Suddenly he was sore clear through. He'd be damned if he would be buffaloed by this man. He turned toward the doorway, as though scared off, then swung about and with three fast, pain-bringing strides was upon Mathison. As he'd anticipated, the mine owner had made the mistake of lowering his revolver. He grabbed the gun by its barrel as Mathison tried to line it on his again. He wrenched it from the man's hand and at the same instant whipped about and slammed against him. Mathison was jolted off balance. He reeled backward, collided with the wall, and slumped there with his red face contorted with rage and his eyes hating Shannon.

"Don't meddle in my affairs again," Shannon said, slapping the words at him. "And don't take that black man's word for whatever it was he told you about me. He's got no more right to that law badge he's wearing than the man in the moon."

A bark of mocking laughter came from the man at the other window. "There never was a lawbreaker who didn't claim he was as innocent as a newborn babe."

Shannon moved away from Mathison and gave that one a sour look. Here was a grizzled old-timer with a gap-toothed grin and snow-white bristles frosting his sunken cheeks. His clothing was hardly better than Shannon's, and his shirt and pants hung baggily on his scrawny frame. His broad-brimmed hat was badly weathered and had long ago lost its shape, while his flat-heeled boots were the worse for wear. Only his eyes retained any trace of the man he once had been; pale blue in color, they were still bright and alert.

He held a long-barreled Colt's revolver in a liver-spotted hand.

"Besides, that's Henry Mathison you're messing with," he went on, this time with cackling laughter. "He's a big, important hombre. Owns half of Lode City. You're asking for more trouble than what you've already got, bucko."

"Don't 'bucko' me, old man," Shannon said, his bad humor persisting. "My name's Shannon. Will Shannon."

"All right, Mr. Will Shannon. Just don't be so touchy with your betters. Hard as you are, the Apaches can lift your hair right along with ours."

"You're the stage driver?"

"That's right. And my name is Hank Dolan. But you don't need to put a mister in front of it."

"You're good at giving advice, Dolan," Shannon said. "But you could use some, yourself. You better get outside and have Harper and Benjy help you move your rig over to the gate before those Apaches come into the gulch."

Dolan looked puzzled. "Why in tarnation should I do that?"

"To block that opening in the wall. So the Apaches can't ride in and over us."

"Now, hold on, you . . . That ain't no mud wagon. It's a Concord coach, and not more than two years old. You know what a rig like that costs?"

Henry Mathison said, "Do as he says, Hank."

His voice had the ring of authority. "He may be a loudmouth, but what he's just said is sensible. Hop to it. Get that gate blocked."

Grumbling, Hank Dolan started toward the doorway.

Shannon faced the pudgy, dapper Shapely. He didn't need to say anything more to him. He just held out his right hand, and the man placed the Winchester in it. At this the woman across the room laughed as though delighted by what she'd witnessed.

Shannon laid Mathison's revolver on the plank table in the middle of the room; then he turned his scowling gaze on her. As he'd noticed upon entering the house, she was flashily attractive. She was wearing a green silk dress with puffed sleeves and a wasp waist that gave her an hour-glass figure. Her hair was piled stylishly atop her head and hennaed an unlikely shade of red. She was not as young as she wanted to appear, for the powder and paint she used failed to hide the ravages of encroaching middle age and loose living. Shannon had her pegged as one of the floozies that always found their way to a booming mining town.

Having stepped on the toes of each of the men, Shannon thought he might as well do things up right by stepping on hers as well.

"Something about me amuses you, ma'am?" he asked, bitingly polite of tone.

Her laughter subsided but the hint of it remained in her voice. "Not you . . . the others. Three big, brave men with guns in their hands cowed by one who didn't even draw his. I'm Belle Larsen, Shannon, if you're curious. I'm always glad to get to know a real man, even if he looks like a tramp. If the Apaches do come, I'll stick close to you."

Mathison burst out, "For God's sake, Belle; the man is a criminal! Don't start playing up to him!"

"My lord and master speaks," the woman said, smiling ruefully. "He has a notion that I belong to him." Then, looking anxious, she asked, "Will they really come here, the Apaches?"

"They'll come," Shannon told her, and he turned to the doorway. From there he added, "You're probably not the praying kind, but if you are . . . well, now is the time to try some prayers for a bunch of poor fools."

He went out, thinking he hadn't done much to set her mind at rest, or to make a friend of her. What ailed him, anyway? It wasn't like him to go around with a chip on his shoulder and falling out with everybody. He was beginning to act like the wrong one that Ben Murdock had made him out to be.

CHAPTER TEN

Limping into the yard with his rifle in the crook of his right arm, Shannon watched the stagecoach being manhandled into position to block the gateway in the adobe wall. Hank Dolan hauled on the tongue while Harper put a shoulder to one rear wheel and Benjy to the other. Ben Murdock was still keeping an eye on the opposite rock wall, from which the sunlight was now gone. Nightfall would come early here in the gulch, but first there would be a period of dusk, a favorite time for Apaches to attack.

When Shannon joined Murdock, the latter said, "A good idea, that." He nodded toward the stagecoach barricade. "I should have thought of it. You're one up on me, ofay."

"If we get through the next hour or so without being hit, we may be safe for the night."

"We may, and we may not."

"You ever hear of Apaches fighting at night?"

"Not that I recall," Murdock said. "But I ain't counting on those red buggers being scared of the dark. So we'll stand watch, you and me. We'll spell each other. These others . . ." He shook his head, looking disgusted. "There's not a good man in the lot."

"That big mining man figures he is," Shannon

said. "But you . . . I thought you were taking a horse and hightailing it."

"I didn't say I wasn't, did I?"

"Could be you're scared you'll ride right into that Delgado and his band of warriors."

Murdock's smile showed gleaming white with a glint of gold. "You're getting to know me too good, Shannon. You're reading my mind. Truth is, I've a bad feeling about this whole business. You ever happen to see Delgado?"

Shannon shook his head. "And I'd rather not happen to see him. Why do you ask?"

"I'm wondering if you know the kind of hombre we're up against," Murdock said. "I saw him twice, the second time when that bunch jumped Sanchez and me in the rock field. I tried my best then to bring him down but couldn't hit him. If I believed in voodoo, like black folks back in Mississippi, I'd figure he's protected by some kind of charm. The first time I ran into him was down in Sonora. I'd heard of a white man living at a Mex village named Zaragosa. His description fitted Phil Amhurst, so I crossed the border. I found the white man, all right, but he didn't in no way look like that slave stealer I was after.

"I stayed on there for a while, those folks being real friendly on account of the gringo dollars I had to spend. I'd get drunk on tequila every night and wake up each morning in some *señorita*'s bed. That tequila . . ." Murdock shuddered and made a face. "You know it's made of worms?"

Shannon shook his head. He prompted, "What about Delgado?"

"Oh, him. . . . Word came that he was raiding in Mexico. He'd just hit a charcoal camp in the mountains close by. Then a column of Mex cavalry showed up. The officer recruited every able-bodied man in the village to go along and fight Delgado. My claiming to be a United States citizen didn't cut no ice. I was hustled off with the others.

"We went marching off, forty soldiers in their pretty uniforms and about thirty of us ragtag irregulars. We searched for three days without finding Delgado. Then he found us. He had about two dozen braves with him, and he cut us to pieces from ambush. Then he led an attack on foot, and it was hand to hand. Delgado stood out among the others because of his size and his being so fierce. After he emptied his rifle, he used his knife. When we broke and ran, he had a ring of dead and wounded Mex around him. He cut the throats of the ones still alive."

"What's this about his size?" Shannon asked.

"He's no ordinary scrawny little Apache, believe me. He's almost as big as I am. And he's got more scars on him than I have. He's got a welt around his neck from when some white men hanged him. They strung him to a propped-up wagon tongue, but he was saved by Geronimo and some others showing up just in time. He was barely alive when they cut him down. He kept that hangman's noose for a souvenir, and he always wears it around his neck when he goes raiding, as a good luck charm."

"A hangman's noose for luck?" Shannon said. "That's loco."

"Not to Delgado," Murdock replied. "To him it's heap big medicine."

"If you're trying to scare me, don't bother," Shannon told him. "I'm always scared when there are Apaches on the loose."

He turned away and went to the stable.

Mrs. Edwards and Tommy were standing well back from the doorway, she holding the boy's hand. Her eyes were anxious and questioning. He looked into their brown depths and shook his head.

"The danger's not over," he said. "It won't be, until that bunch of Apaches is run down by the army. Come along to the house now. It's safe enough to cross the yard."

He kept close to her and the boy, on the side toward the far wall. He had some thought of shielding them with his own body if any more shots came from up there.

Tommy said, "Will soldiers come here?" His voice was full of hope for excitement to come. "Will I see them?"

"I'd like to see a couple of troops of cavalry,

myself, son," Shannon said. "Better them than the Apaches."

"Aw, you'll take care of them old Indians now that you've got your guns. You and the sheriff. Won't you?"

"We'll sure try," Shannon said.

When they reached the house, Mrs. Edwards said, "I haven't forgotten that cup of coffee. If you'll wait a moment . . ."

He managed a smile. "I won't be going anywhere, ma'am."

"I'll stay here with him," Tommy said. Then, as his mother forcibly took him with her, he complained, "Golly wallopers, I can't do nothing!"

She returned shortly, bringing not only the coffee but also a tin plate laden with beans, bacon, and biscuits.

"That sure looks good, Mrs. Edwards," he said, accepting the unexpected meal. "I'm obliged to you."

He seated himself on the bench to one side of the doorway, placed the cup of coffee beside him, and picked up the fork from the plate. He hadn't realized until this moment how hungry he was. The venison Murdock had given him earlier hadn't stayed with him. He looked at the woman.

"Has the black man been fed?"

"He helped himself right after the two of you

arrived," she said, "when he took the guns inside. He should have given a thought to the possibility that you would be hungry, too."

"Oh, he and I don't hit it off. We're not exactly friends."

Smiling, she said, "I can imagine that you're not."

She went back inside, and he gave his attention to the food.

Dusk had come and was rapidly deepening into darkness. Harper, Benjy, and Dolan went to the house. Ben Murdock had given up watching the rim of the wall and gone outside, climbing over the stagecoach, to prowl the gulch. When he finished his meal, Shannon took his empty plate and cup into the house and left them on the table. The lantern there had been lighted, and a lamp burned in the kitchen too. Everybody was gathered back there, evidently for supper. He picked up his saddlebags and took them outside with some notion of shaving and cleaning up.

Murdock was returning. Joining him, Shannon asked, "Find anything?"

"I didn't see anything," the other man said. "But there's no law saying that the Apaches have got to let us see them coming. They could sneak up on us. There's plenty of brush and rocks for cover."

"That's a pleasant thought. One thing you should do, you being the man in authority, is organize our defenses. It's not enough just you and I spelling each other at standing guard."

"Organize them how?"

"You should be able to figure out what should be done," Shannon said, a bite to his voice. "A man wearing a badge is expected to handle trouble when it comes along, any kind of trouble."

Grinning, Murdock said, "I'm new at the job. You'll have to give me a helping hand."

"Well, as a starter you should find out how many guns Harper has around the place. Maybe he has another rifle or two, maybe even a shotgun. Hank Dolan and Henry Mathison will do better with long guns than with revolvers. And you should get a supply of water laid in, on the chance that Delgado will lay siege to the station."

"Sounds reasonable. Anything else?"

"They've got lights burning inside," Shannon said. "Tell them to put them out as soon as they can. No sense in keeping a light in the window for a bunch of hostiles. And see if the doors can be barred. If they can't, they'll have to be barricaded when and if we come under attack."

"I'll take care of things," Murdock said. "If you see or hear anything, let loose with a shot. I'll come running."

Alone, Shannon climbed to the top of the stagecoach for a better view of the approaches to the station. He seated himself cross-legged with his rifle across his thighs, and again he had the feeling of being penned in, trapped, here in the gulch. He felt in his pockets for makings and found a little Bull Durham and some papers. He rolled and lighted a cigarette. A moment later, intent upon watching beyond the station wall, he was startled by someone climbing the coach. Looking down, he saw it was the boy.

"You, Tommy: get back to your ma . . . pronto!"

"I want to keep watch with you," the boy said, reaching the front boot. "I've got my gun. See?" He held up his wooden revolver. "And I'm a real good shot." After a pause, he added, "Shucks, it ain't a real gun. But if it was I'd sure shoot somebody. You know who?"

"I sure don't. Who would you?"

"That Mr. Mathison, that's who," Tommy said.

He climbed to the driver's seat and knelt there. Seeing the intent look on his small face, Shannon realized with a sense of shock that the boy was serious.

"Why would you want to do a bad thing like that to Mr. Mathison?"

"Because he's to blame for my pa getting killed."

"Oh, that can't be."

"It is, though. I heard Ma say it right after Pa was killed. She said it to the lady who lived next door to us. She was crying something awful when she said it. She didn't know I heard it, but I did."

Shannon didn't know what to say to that. After

a moment he said, “Listen, son: you’re the only man your ma has now, and you shouldn’t do anything to upset her.”

“I never do, and, golly gee, that’s the truth.”

“I’m glad to hear it,” Shannon said. “But if she misses you, while you’re out here in the dark, she’ll be plenty upset. Now you go back to the house. You and I will talk some more in the morning. All right?”

The boy considered that, finally saying, “I guess I’ll go. It’s kind of spooky out here, anyway.”

He climbed down from the coach and scampered to the house.

Time passed, and Shannon continued to keep watch alone. He heard an occasional voice raised in anger over at the house, which he took to be that of Henry Mathison. He thought this a fine time for Ben Murdock to get into an argument with the mine owner. Or vice versa. On second thought, he doubted that the black man would take any guff off Mathison.

He saw one of the women appear at the doorway and stand there for a moment, limned against the lantern light within. When she walked in his direction, he realized it was Mrs. Edwards. He experienced a little stir of excitement. Climbing down from the coach, he mocked himself with the thought that she wasn’t likely to appreciate his reacting to her in such a manner.

"Something wrong?" he asked.

"No, not really." She had a shawl about her shoulders in anticipation of the coming night chill. "I managed to get Tommy settled down for the night, and I felt that I must get out for a breath of air. With everyone crowded into the house, it's becoming stuffy. And noisy. They get to arguing."

"That would be Mathison and the black man?"

"Yes."

"What's their point of dispute?"

"Mr. Mathison says that the deputy should ride for help," she said. "He reasons that it's Mr. Murdock's duty, since he is a lawman. He feels that Mr. Murdock can bring troops in time to save us from attack."

"And Murdock?"

"He argues that he will be needed here."

"He'll go," Shannon said, more to himself than to her. "He wants to be talked into it, so he can go with a clear conscience."

She looked at him uncertainly but did not ask for an explanation. Moving to the wall, she looked down through the gulch. He followed and stood beside her, becoming sharply aware of her nearness. He found her more desirable each time he was with her. Despite the darkness, he could see that her face was grave and touched by sorrow. She had the memory of her husband with her now, and because of that she was not at the moment fearful.

But she had not put the threat of an Apache attack wholly out of her thoughts, for she said, “It’s so very dark. How will you see them if they come?”

“I’ve always heard that they don’t fight at night. They are said to believe that the spirit of a warrior killed in the dark doesn’t go to the happy hunting ground. I’m hoping there’s some truth to that.”

She was silent for a time, seeming to think about what he had said. Finally she said, “It’s a childish belief, isn’t it? But they are a primitive people. Do you suppose it comes of a fear of the dark, such a belief?”

“That could be,” Shannon said. “My guess is that all peoples came by their beliefs because of fear of something or other, away back when they were primitive and gullible. Fear of goblins or demons or devils. A bit ago I told the other lady here to do some praying, but my own beliefs are pretty shaky. I always put my trust in this Winchester rifle.”

Mrs. Edwards seemed a bit shocked. She said rebukingly, “Some people would say that you’re being . . . well, blasphemous.” She was silent for a moment, thoughtful. “Still, I myself have of late come to doubt the beliefs I was taught as a child. I’ve become bitter, I suppose. And cynical.

I wonder why a good man should die so young, while others . . .”

As her voice faltered, Shannon said, “Life is mighty unfair, Mrs. Edwards. What caused the accident that took your husband’s life?”

“The miserliness of the mine’s owner,” she said, and her voice was edged with her bitterness. “My husband was the mine superintendent. He kept demanding that more timbering be placed in the tunnels and drifts. The owner refused to spend the necessary money. And there was a cave-in.”

“That mine owner is Henry Mathison?”

“Yes, Henry Mathison.” Her voice was charged with hatred now. “I blame him. I feel that he killed my husband and the other men who died at the same time, killed them to save what to him would have been very little money. Not as much, I imagine, as he spends on that Larsen woman in a few months. If I had known he was traveling on this stagecoach, I certainly wouldn’t have taken it. I can’t bear the sight of him. Is that petty of me, Mr. Shannon?”

“You’ve a right to feel the way you do, I’d say. Where are you bound, ma’am?”

“Back East to Philadelphia, which was my home before I married. My sister, who is my only living relative, has offered to let Tommy and me live with her and her family until I can find a way to earn a livelihood. I dislike taking advantage of her good nature, but I have no choice. I was at my wit's end until I received her letter. I used up almost all the money my husband and I had put aside for a rainy day. There was barely enough left for the stage and train fares."

"You received no compensation from Mathison?"

"He offered me a hundred dollars. In my anger I refused it."

"Have you something in mind to work at?"

"If you mean am I trained for some work, no, I'm not. I don't know what I'll do."

Her voice had taken on a tone of anxiety, and he sensed that she was facing the future with little hope and a courage that was faltering. He silently damned the Henry Mathisons of this world. They built their fortunes on the suffering of others.

"Forgive me for crying on your shoulder," she said, turning to him with a rueful smile. "After all, you have troubles of your own."

"Mine will work out," he said. "Things aren't exactly as Murdock has told you and the others."

She gazed at him with curiosity. "I find myself wondering about you, Mr. Shannon. About what sort of man you are."

"I'm a pretty ordinary sort. So call me 'Will,' why don't you?"

"All right . . . Will. My name is Helen. Would I be too nosy if I asked why you're under arrest?"

This, he realized, was the moment to clear himself, at least in her eyes. But, before he had a chance to speak, an alien sound reached him through the quiet night. He laid a cautioning hand on her arm and peered one way and another down the gulch. He heard nothing more and saw nothing, but he sensed that someone was out there in the deep darkness.

"What is it, Will?"

"They've come," he said. "Go to the house and tell Murdock we've got company."

"The Apaches?"

"Yes, the Apaches," he said. "Get going, damn it!"

His brusqueness started her running across the yard.

He saw them now. Three shadowy horsemen were moving slowly, warily down into the gulch. Behind them came a dozen others. Delgado had arrived . . . with enough warriors to overrun anything less than a troop of cavalry.

CHAPTER ELEVEN

They approached from the south, and Shannon took up a position at the wall on that side of the yard. No sense of bravado bolstered his courage. He was primed to fight only because there was no choice. He had no belief that Delgado and his warriors could be held off. He had only a hope that Murdock and he would hurt them so badly that they would decide that taking the station was not worth the cost in Apache lives.

Murdock came running, making only a whisper of sound. He breasted the adobe wall and peered into the darkness. When he turned, Shannon saw that the whites of his eyes showed all around. He realized then that the black man too could know fear.

In a barely audible whisper Murdock asked, "What are you waiting for, ofay?"

"I wouldn't know," Shannon said, also whispering. "Maybe to see if they've come to smoke the peace pipe. Shall we start the fandango?"

"Let them get closer. They'll be easier targets."

The first three Indians halted at the bottom of the grade and were now on a level with the station. The main part of the band stopped a hundred feet or so farther back, on slightly higher ground.

"That's about it," Murdock said. "They'll dismount and take cover now. Let's give them a welcome. My hunch is that the buck in the middle, up front, is Delgado. You take him."

"Why me," Shannon asked, "when your Sharps reaches farther and hits harder?"

Murdock said, "Voodoo. He's got a charm that works against me. Maybe it's not good against you."

"You superstitious black bugger," Shannon said, and lined his Winchester's sights on the shadowy figure Murdock believed to be Delgado.

He squeezed off his shot, and missed. The Apache he'd tried to down let out a defiant yell and brandished his rifle. The others began howling and for a moment milled about in confusion. Shannon fired again, with no more luck. Murdock's buffalo gun added its thunderclap report to the din.

At a command from Delgado all but two of the Apaches dismounted and scattered among the brush and rocks. The two still mounted drove the riderless ponies out of the gulch. Within seconds not a single warrior was to be seen.

"Now we know," Shannon said. "They'll fight in the dark, all right."

"They would have, if they'd be able to take us by surprise," Murdock said. "You'll notice they haven't fired a shot yet. One thing sure, ofay, your Winchester is no better than my Sharps against Delgado. It must be that hangman's noose that keeps him safe."

"If you believe that, you'll believe that the moon is made of green cheese."

"Nobody'll ever prove it ain't."

"That's one thing sure," Shannon said. "When are you taking a horse and heading out?"

Chuckling, Murdock said, "Any time now. That loud-talking mining man, Mathison, argues that it's my duty to go. Who am I to call a big, important man like him a liar?"

"I'll tell you something, you woman-murdering bastard: you're not riding out. I'll shoot any bronc you mount."

"Even if there was a chance that I could bring help?"

"You know damn well there's no chance of that. And because there's not, you're staying to help fight. And if we manage to drive them off, unlikely though that is, I'll be taking you to Valido to hang."

"That again," Murdock said. "Ofay, you've sure got a one-track mind. You see anything of them redskins?"

"You're the one with the cat's eyes. Do you see them?"

"Nope. They must have tucked themselves in nice and comfy for the night."

A man came scurrying across the yard from the now dark and silent house. He was bent low, to make a smaller target of himself. He crouched against the wall. It was the stage driver, Dolan.

"Did they pull out?"

"No, they've gone to ground," Murdock said. "Maybe to wait for daylight or maybe to get up the nerve to fight in the dark. What about the folks inside? Are they sleeping through it?"

"Mr. Big Man Mathison and the drummer are at the windows, ready to defend the women and children with their last drop of blood." Dolan spat tobacco juice to show his contempt for those two. "Mel Harper is hitting the jug, to jack up his nerve. Benjy and the boy are bedded down, sleeping the sleep of the young and innocent. The two women are just waiting and hoping. And maybe praying, for all the good that'll do. How many Injuns?"

"More than a dozen," Shannon said, "one of them Delgado."

"That means we have as much chance as a gelded jack mule in a herd of jennies," Dolan said, and he rose for a cautious look over the wall.

That instant rifle fire erupted from several different spots out there, leaving Shannon and Murdock with no need to wonder longer if Apaches would fight in the dark. Counting the muzzle flashes, Shannon found that only four of the band were shooting. Their target was the station house; a shattering of window panes could be heard along with the racket of shots.

Delgado was wily indeed, Shannon realized as he prepared to fire at one of the muzzle flashes. The Apache leader hadn't yet spotted Shannon and his companions at the wall, and he was holding most of his weapons in reserve for when the return fire came. Which was now, for Dolan started shooting with his revolver and Ben Murdock's buffalo gun added its thunderclap report to the din.

After Shannon squeezed off his first shot, the entire south end of the gulch came alive with spurts of powder flame that glared against the darkness. Shannon knew that Indians had no great reputation for marksmanship; generally their shooting was wild and wasteful. But Delgado and his warriors were as disciplined in their use of firearms as well-trained troops. They fired with care, slowly and methodically, and every Apache gun out there was now turned on Shannon and his companions.

Slugs shrieked past their heads. Others thudded into the adobe wall. Hank Dolan cried out and went down. Out among the rocks and brush a warrior let loose with a blood-curdling scream that told he had been hit. Another reared up into full view, took a few staggering steps, and then collapsed.

Shannon and Murdock ducked down after each shot, moving this way and that along the wall before rising to fire again. This maneuvering gave them a slight advantage, but they were still constantly close to death. A slug kicked adobe dirt from the wall into Shannon's face, and Murdock swore as a bullet snatched away his hat. The barrel of Shannon's Winchester grew hot to his touch. He had the stink of burnt black powder in his nostrils and the taste of it in his mouth. The unpleasant thought came to him that the Apaches, with the law of averages in their favor, had only to continue their shooting to do for him and Murdock.

We're not hurting them enough. . . . They're too hard to get at.

Although a wily tactician, Delgado evidently knew nothing about the law of averages, for the shooting ceased abruptly. The sudden silence was jarring. It left Shannon on edge, waiting tensely for the shooting to resume. As the silence stretched on, he peered into the darkness with another disquieting thought gripping him.

They'll rush us now.

Shoving fresh loads from his pocket into the Winchester's magazine, he said, "If they come at us, we're goners."

"Unless we can drop enough of them once they're in the open," Murdock replied. "So far, we've nailed only two of them. That's mighty poor shooting."

Minutes passed, and no howling, shooting

warriors came charging through the darkness.

Finally Murdock said, "They've got a bellyful for now. They're pulling back."

Shannon saw first one and then another obscure shape dart from brush clump to brush clump and from rock to rock, away from the Apaches' positions. A third went off in the same furtive manner, then a fourth. They were indeed withdrawing. Delgado had missed his chance, let opportunity slip through his fingers. Shannon heaved an audible sigh of relief.

"Don't feel so good about it," Murdock told him. "They won't go far. We'll have them to deal with again at dawn."

Shannon didn't argue the point, but he said, "We could nail some of them now, and there'd be fewer to come back later."

"Help yourself, if you're of a mind to kill the poor bastards," Murdock said. "Me, I'm not . . . not when they're not shooting at me." Seeing Shannon's wondering look, he went on, "I've got a feeling for Indians. Like black folks, they've suffered plenty because of the whites. Only difference between them and my kind is that they didn't make good enough slaves. But they lost their freedom and their land all the same, and now they're supposed to live half-starved on reservations and be peaceable. All these Apaches ever wanted was to keep you damn white-eyes from stealing their country away from them.

They weren't able to do it, but you can't rightly blame them for going on a rampage once in a while and trying to get even."

Shannon watched another shadowy figure dart away and leave the gulch. He made no attempt to line his sights on the warrior.

"That's one way of looking at it," he said, "but a damn fool way when it's your life they're gunning for."

"It's the only way to look at it," Murdock said. And then, with a grin, he added, "It is when they're not shooting at an hombre, anyway."

Shannon didn't reply to that. He turned to the downed stage driver. Dolan was seated on the ground, his left hand gripping his right shoulder. Blood seeped between his fingers. His wizened old face had taken on a dull-witted expression, as though he was in a state of shock.

Shannon said, "I'll get somebody to take you inside and patch you up, Hank," and strode to the house. Finding the door shut and barred, he pounded on it with his fist.

"Open up! We've got a wounded man out here!"

Somebody opened the door a scant inch and peered out with one eye. "What do you want?"

Recognizing the curt, arrogant voice of Henry Mathison, Shannon felt his hackles rise. He could hate this man more than he did the Apaches.

"Is everybody all right in there?" he asked.

"So far, yes. Did you drive those bastards off?"

"They called it off for the time being," Shannon said. "You and Harper or the drummer come out and give Dolan a hand. He's been hit."

He turned away at once, going back to the wall.

Mathison sent the drummer, Shapely, and the station agent, Harper, to take Hank Dolan to the house. That was to be expected, Shannon thought sourly. Henry Mathison wasn't one to stoop to menial labor even if it was merely the carrying of a wounded man a few yards. He was far too important. The mine owner did venture into the yard, however, after Shapely and Harper had taken Dolan inside. He held his short-barreled revolver in his hand and was visibly nervous.

"You're sure they're gone, are you?" he demanded of Murdock. "They're tricky devils. They could be planning to pull something."

"They've cleared out of the gulch," Murdock told him. "But that doesn't mean they've given up on us. My hunch is that they'll hit us again at dawn."

"By then a rider could be at Tucson, getting word out to the military as to how desperate the situation here is."

"If you mean that rider should be me, boss, you can just forget it." Murdock's voice held dislike of the mine owner; he made no attempt to hide his ill feeling for Mathison. "Like I told you before, I'm needed here. Another thing, Shannon here has threatened to shoot any horse I fork."

Mathison gave Shannon a look of contempt, then turned back to the black man. "What kind of a lawman are you, anyway, letting your prisoner make such a threat? You made a mighty stupid move when you took the handcuffs off him and let him arm himself. You'd better take his guns, now that the danger is over for the time being. He could shoot you in the back and run for it."

"You try to take his guns, Mathison . . . and see what it gets you."

"Are you admitting you're afraid of him?"

"I'm plenty scared of him, up to a certain point."

Mathison swore under his breath with the anger of a man unaccustomed to having others refuse to carry out his orders. "If you won't go for help, Ed Shapely will," he said. "I've offered him a thousand dollars to go, and he's agreed to try it, provided the Apaches have pulled back. I'll have Harper get a mount ready for him."

"White man, you may be rich but you ain't God," Murdock said. "Quit messing around with other men's lives."

Mathison swore again. "Use a civil tongue when you talk to me, Deputy. Any man in a position to pay someone what amounts to a small fortune to ride forty or fifty miles deserves respect, not condemnation. Shapely is not only eager to earn that thousand dollars, he's anxious to get away from here, to save himself."

Shannon decided to put in his two-cents worth. "Friend, you talk loco. Shapely is a city man and probably doesn't know the head end of a horse from the tail end. Another thing, the only horse broke to the saddle is that stove-in chestnut. It wouldn't carry a man ten miles between now and sunup."

"Shapely grew up on a Pennsylvania farm and rode horses as a boy," Mathison said, his voice loud and domineering. "And Harper says that he's ridden one of the company horses, a sorrel gelding. There's no reason in the world that Shapely can't make it safely."

"No reason except there may be Apaches north of here as well as south . . . for him to run into," Shannon said. "Our not having seen any in that direction doesn't mean none are there."

He'd had his say, and he wanted no further part in the argument. He walked to the house and found the door no longer barred. Entering, he saw Hank Dolan seated on a bench at the plank table. The lantern was burning again with a low flame. The stage driver, with both his shirt and his undershirt off, appeared to be only skin and bones. Belle Larsen was wrapping a bandage about his wounded arm, while Helen Edwards was clearing away some bloodstained rags and a basin in which the water had turned pink.

Dolan held a tin cup in his left hand, which he raised to Shannon. "Women and whiskey," he said gleefully. "My idea of heaven. I ain't had such a fuss made over me in forty years." He drank from the cup, then grinned up at Belle and winked at Shannon. "It was worth getting shot for. You should try it, bucko."

Mathison's woman gave Shannon a patently flirtatious look. "Mrs. Edwards and I have it all planned for him, Hank. Now that the danger is over she and I are going to give him a scrubbing with yellow soap and then shave him, make him respectable. Isn't that right, Helen?"

Forcing a smile but not looking at all amused, Helen Edwards said, "I'm sure Mr. Shannon will make himself respectable when he has time."

She went off to the kitchen to dispose of the messy things left from the treating of Dolan's wound.

Belle Larsen looked after her and made a face. "Respectable ladies . . . no sense of humor. Shannon, what *do* you look like cleaned up?"

Giving her a stingy grin, he said, "Real handsome." Then, sobering, he asked, "How bad was Hank hit?"

"A crease, Harper called it," she said. "It looked nasty enough to me. A lot of blood. I wouldn't have thought the old man had so much left in him."

"I'm not over the hill yet, woman," Dolan said. "Don't think for a second I am!"

That was the whiskey talking, Shannon knew. With that in mind, he went to the kitchen and found, as he had expected, Mel Harper and Ed Shapely seated at the table guzzling whiskey from tin cups. The jug stood by Harper's elbow. Shannon reached for it, and the station agent, quite drunk, tried to grab it from him.

"What do you think you're doing?" Harper's face, with its shaggy beard and red clown's nose, took on a pugnacious scowl. "For a man on his way to Yuma Prison, you're sure taking a lot on yourself."

"I warned you to go on the wagon," Shannon told him. "Now I'm making sure that you do."

Harper set his cup aside and heaved to his feet. He kicked the bench aside, toppling it over, and made a lurching, belligerent move in Shannon's direction. He laid a hand on his revolver and made a fumbling draw.

"By damn, I'll show you who's boss around here!"

Shannon swung his rifle and rapped him hard on the forearm. Harper dropped his gun, let out a yelp of pain, and reeled backward. Shannon eyed him narrowly for a moment. Seeing that the fight had gone out of Harper, he shifted his gaze to the chubby Ed Shapely.

"Just how drunk are you, friend?"

The drummer managed to replace the vacuous look on his pudgy face with an expression of indignation. “You, sir, are being insulting. I can hold my liquor and—”

“Whether you’re drunk or sober, I’ll give you some advice you’d better heed,” Shannon broke in. “Don’t let Mathison talk you into riding for help for any amount of money. You’d never get past the Apaches, and heaven help you if they should take you alive. If Mathison brings the matter up again, you ask him why he doesn’t go.”

“Listen, mister: it’s none of your business what I—”

Shannon didn’t wait to hear the rest of it. He left the kitchen, taking the jug with him. Helen followed him through the main room, where the Larsen woman was helping Hank Dolan back into his undershirt. He held the door open, and Helen went out ahead of him. Henry Mathison passed them on his way inside. His face in the dim light from within was so stiff with anger it might have been chiseled out of red stone. He had no word for either Shannon or the woman, nor they for him.

Helen remained just outside the doorway, but Shannon moved out from the house to upend the jug and pour its contents onto the thirsty soil.

Murdock loomed out of the dark, saying, “That’s a sinful waste.”

“You want a pull at it?”

"I could do with a small one."

Shannon handed him the jug, and the other man drank from it in the approved manner. With his thumb in the handle, he posed the jug on his raised upper arm and put his mouth to the neck. After drinking deeply, he handed it back to Shannon, who poured off what remained. He tossed the empty jug to the side of the house.

"Harper will sure try to square that with you," Murdock said. He took two long, slender Mexican cigars from his shirt pocket and offered one to Shannon. "Smoke, ofay?"

Shannon accepted the cigar, as well as a light from the match the black man struck. "Where did you come by these?" he asked.

"That boozer has a sackful," Murdock said. "I helped myself to them, figuring he owes me for keeping the Apaches from lifting his scalp and burning his station." He glanced at Helen and then looked knowingly back at Shannon. "I believe the lady wants your company. I'll go back and stand guard."

Shannon turned to the woman. "Is there something?"

"Yes . . . yes, there is. Will you walk with me, please?"

Smiling and giving her a little bow, he said, "My pleasure, ma'am."

He walked beside her, letting her choose the pace and direction. She moved slowly across the yard and stopped beside the well. She shivered visibly and drew her shawl closer about herself. He wondered at her being cold. The night was cooling but not yet really chill. He thought it unlikely that she still was gripped by fear, now that the Apaches were not an immediate threat. Something had upset her, he decided; something other than the brief fight with Delgado and his warriors.

Facing him, she said, "Tell me truthfully . . . could a rider get past the Apaches?"

"Not if the rider was Ed Shapely."

"If it were you?"

"I?" he said, startled. "Well, maybe I could, with the devil's own luck. But if I made it past them I couldn't get back with help soon enough. The Apaches will hit us again at dawn, and—"

"I wasn't thinking of your getting back with help," she said. Her face was a white oval in the darkness; it seemed to have taken on a deep pallor. And it was set with purpose. "If I helped you get away from the deputy," she went on, "would you take Tommy with you . . . so he will be safe?"

He stared at her mutely, so taken by surprise he didn't know what to say.

"I have a derringer pistol in my reticule," she said, and her voice hinted at the desperation gripping her. "I could use it to force Mr. Murdock to give up his guns to you. Then you could take a horse. . . .” She began to sob. “Oh, please! I don’t want my little boy to die here, at the hands of those savages!”

Shannon stared at her with dismay now, knowing he must refuse to do as she asked but not how to word his refusal so that she would not become even more upset. He feared that Helen Edwards was already on the verge of hysteria.

CHAPTER TWELVE

Taking Shannon's silence as his answer, Helen Edwards said, "You won't do it. You won't even try to save yourself. I don't understand you. I don't, at all."

Her tone was despairing, but otherwise she seemed to have firm hold of herself. Instead of becoming more agitated, as he had feared, she seemed more calm. He realized that she had simply resigned herself to the fact that she could not get her son safely away. As she turned from him, Shannon laid a hand on her arm and stopped her.

For a moment he did not speak but gazed mutely at her pale face. He was gripped by an almost overpowering urge to take her in his arms and try to comfort her as a man would his own woman.

When he spoke it was with more feeling than was his habit. "This situation isn't as it seems. I could leave here anytime, and Murdock wouldn't try to stop me. He's not a lawman, and I'm not his prisoner . . . at least, not when I'm armed."

She gazed at him with what he took to be disbelief.

"But that's neither here nor there," he went on. "The thing is, if I rode out and ran into Apaches

I'd have to fight to get past them. And with the boy along I wouldn't be able to put up a fight. We would both die out there."

Helen said nothing. She continued to stare at him, trancelike.

"I want Tommy to be safe," he said. "But I want you to live through this, too. And the other woman. The men as well, poor excuses for men though they are. As for Murdock, I've a special reason for wanting him to get away from here alive."

Helen spoke at last, tonelessly. "You can't keep us safe, and you know it. If you stay, you won't even be able to save yourself. We'll all die here . . . horribly."

She had completely despaired. In trying to reassure her, he spoke more harshly than he had intended.

"Damn it, woman; it's not all that hopeless. Murdock and I have fought this same band of hostiles. I had a fight with five of Delgado's warriors a few days ago, and I survived. He came through a fight with the main portion of the band a day later. Together he and I fought them to a standstill tonight. There's a chance that we can stop them when they attack this station again."

A slim chance, he thought; a very slim chance.

Helen said, "You are only two, against so many."

"The others will back us up," he told her.

"Mathison, Shapely, and Harper. Those three can't just sit back on their hands when the Apaches come right up to the wall. At any rate, I haven't given up hope. Neither has Murdock. This is the best way, believe me. And don't think ill of me for not doing as you want."

"I won't do that," she said spiritlessly as she turned away.

After he walked to the house with her, he rejoined Murdock.

"What do you think? Will they be back again tonight?"

"My hunch is, they won't."

"Then I'll leave you to keep watch for a while," Shannon said. "I've got something to do."

"Now what would that be?"

Shannon rubbed a hand over his face. His cheeks and chin felt like prickly pear cactus. "I'm going to get cleaned up. I'm tired of looking like a saddle tramp."

Chuckling, Murdock said, "A handsome woman, the widow. I was wondering if you'd noticed."

Shannon said, "To hell with you, Murdock," and went to the stagecoach, where he'd left his saddlebags.

Going to the stable he lit a lantern, keeping the flame low, and took two buckets he found there to the well. Returning with the water, he dug a cake of yellow soap from his saddlebags, stripped down, and scrubbed himself from head to foot. His underwear was too rank for further wear, so he left it off and pulled on his pants and boots. He got out his razor, honed it on the sole of his left boot, then worked up a lather on his stubbly face. Shaving without a mirror was a tricky business, and he kept nicking himself, drawing blood, as he scraped at his wiry beard.

Someone entered the stable. After a moment a voice said, "You'll cut your throat if you're not careful."

Recognizing the voice as Belle Larsen's, he looked over his shoulder. She came to stand in the faint glow of the lantern. She smiled at him as she had earlier, flirtatiously. Despite her hennaed hair and trollop's painted face, she was an attractive woman. She was also, he reflected, a dangerous one.

Civil of tone but no more than that, he said, "Listen, lady: you may be willing to risk trouble with Mathison, but I'm not. Why don't you be sensible and go back to the house?"

"Henry Mathison only thinks he owns me," she said, "and he couldn't be more wrong. The truth is, Shannon, he's not half the man he believes. Now you . . . you're looking better by the second. Just go ahead with your shaving."

"Your being here makes me nervous. It could cause me to cut my throat."

"What a waste of a good man that would be."

"You don't know I'm that. And you're not likely to find out, under the circumstances. Good-bye to you, Miss Larsen."

Making a face at him, she said, "You prefer that oh-so-proper widow? Forget it, Shannon. She's not likely to be interested, and she wouldn't be right for you if she were. What you need in a woman is—"

He ignored the rest of what she said, turning his back and going on with his shaving. Since his plying the razor by touch alone required considerable concentration, he was only vaguely aware when she left him. He finished shaving, laid the razor aside, and splashed water over his face. He found himself feeling like a new man.

As he took his spare shirt from the saddlebags, he became aware that someone had again entered the stable. Thinking it was the Larsen woman returning, he looked around and said, "What now?" Then, staring, he burst out, "What the hell?"

This time it wasn't Belle Larsen but Mel Harper, and with him Ed Shapely. The station agent carried an ax handle, and his bearded face wore a wickedly amused grin. Shannon turned in alarm to a pile of sacked grain upon which he had left his rifle and gun rig. They were no longer there, and he realized that the Larsen woman had taken them. She had made sure he would be unable to shoot Harper when the agent used that ax handle on him. But why? What was it all about?

He was given no answers. Harper said gleefully, "Now I'll show you who's boss around here, hombre," and lunged at him with the handle raised for a clubbing blow.

Shannon tried to dodge away and then to come close to the agent, but his injured knee made his movements sluggish. And Harper was one of those men most dangerous when drunk. With alcoholic cunning he feinted a blow with his club, and then, as Shannon came closer, Harper lashed out at his head. Shannon threw up a shielding arm, but too late. He was struck with tremendous force at the left side of his head. Pain burst all through him. He was knocked off his feet, and he lay, in a crumpled heap, stunned to the point of helplessness.

A slender thread of consciousness remained to him, and he was dimly aware that Harper tied his hands behind him and afterward gave him a vicious kick in the ribs. With this second explosion of pain he was content to let his consciousness slip away. When he regained his senses, he found Ben Murdock bending over him.

"And you and me," the black man said, "figured ourselves a couple of tough hands." He cut Shannon's bonds and helped him sit up. "How'd they manage to hog-tie you, ofay?"

"That red-headed floozy took my guns while I

was shaving, then Harper used an ax handle on me. Where were you when they jumped me?"

"Mathison got a shotgun from Harper and held it on me with both triggers cocked," Murdock said. "I figured he was loco enough to cut me in half if I batted an eye. So I 'yas-sahed' him all over the place and let him take my guns."

"What was it all about?"

"Can't you guess?"

Shannon had an idea. "They figured you and I would keep Shapely from riding out. Has he gone?"

"About a minute ago. The others gave him three cheers and wished him bon voyage. The horse Harper gave him tried to throw him, but he stuck like a burr."

Struggling to his feet and rubbing the left side of his head, Shannon said, "Well, here's hoping he makes it."

He'd hardly gotten those words out when a flurry of shots sounded in the distance. Half a dozen shots, and then silence. Shannon stared at Murdock, and the black man stared back at him.

"Too bad," Murdock said. "Take another wish, this one that he's dead."

Anger swept through Shannon, turning his freshly shaven face ugly. In low, savage tones, he cursed Henry Mathison, Mel Harper, and Belle Larsen.

When he fell silent and reached for his shirt,

Ben Murdock said, “My sentiments exactly.” He sounded disgusted.

Mathison entered the stable but stopped a cautious distance from Shannon and Murdock. He still carried the shotgun. He seemed to have lost some of his arrogance. His heavy red face wore a troubled frown. Mel Harper appeared behind him, looking sheepish.

Shannon gazed at the pair with his anger flaring up again. “Well, you got the poor fool killed,” he said, his tone not just accusing but condemning. “The two of you must be mighty proud of yourselves.”

Mathison’s expression turned sullen. “He wanted to go. Nobody forced him. You’re not making me feel guilty about it.”

“No more guilty than you felt about the men who died in that cave-in because you wouldn’t spend a little money to timber your mine,” Shannon said. “Your kind never feel guilty about anything, because, like Murdock said a while back, men like you believe they’re God Almighty.”

Mathison made a threatening gesture with the shotgun. “I’ll stand for no more such talk, Shannon. Not from you. I don’t have to. I’m a man of standing in this world, and you . . . you’re a nothing. Now get back to the wall and keep watch. And you, Deputy, get back there with him.”

"Whatever you say, sir," Murdock said, making a show of a darky's bowing and scraping. "You're the boss, sure enough. A big, important man. You're so big and important it wonders me that the Apaches got the nerve to shoot up this place while you're here. But what about our guns, Mr. Boss Man? We sure can't fight them redskins with our bare hands."

"You'll get your guns back when and if the Apaches attack us again," Mathison said. "Now move, damn it . . . the two of you!"

Shannon tucked his shirttails into his pants, donned his hat, and buckled on his gun rig with its empty holster. He moved toward the doorway, walking wide around Mathison. He noticed that the mine owner had neither of the shotgun's triggers cocked. With that Shannon let his anger erupt into action. He lunged at the man, slamming against him and getting a one-handed hold on the gun. Mathison stood firm and drove a fist to his ribs that still ached from Harper's kick, causing him to grunt with a fresh spasm of pain.

Struggling against each other for possession of the weapon, they traded punches with their free hands. Mathison had sufficient bulk to stagger Shannon a time or two, but it was brawn turned flabby and he was unable to absorb the hard blows dealt him. Shannon battered him with a savagery born of rage and hatred, alternating his punches between the man's soft midsection and his ruddy face. Mathison's eyes took on a glazed look, and his breathing became a labored gasping. Finally his hold on the shotgun weakened, and Shannon wrenched the weapon from his hand.

Mathison uttered a bellow of rage and moved at a lumbering run to the opposite side of the stable. He returned at once, charging at Shannon with a pitchfork. The sharp tines of the fork glinted menacingly in the dim lantern light. Mathison let out another bellow. He was a man gone berserk.

Murdock yelled, "Use that scatter-gun, ofay! Drop him, you fool!"

Shannon made no attempt to shoot. He ducked aside, and Mathison, missing him with the pitchfork, drove its tines deep into a sack of grain. Before the mine owner could wrench it free for another thrust, Shannon struck him at the base of the skull with the shotgun. Mathison lost his hold on the fork and collapsed to his hands and knees. He remained in that position, seeming too dazed to rise.

Turning to meet a possible attack by Mel Harper, Shannon saw that Murdock had the agent backed against the wall and was taking his revolver from him. Harper's bearded face was contorted by fear. He huddled against the wall, staring wide eyed at the gun as Murdock raised it for a blow.

"Don't! It was all his doing, not mine!"

Murdock lowered the revolver, turned to

Shannon, and said, "I'm leaving this place . . . saving myself." His voice was harsh with anger. "Why should I side these bastards? If you've got any sense at all, you'll clear out, too."

Shannon shook his head. "We'd never make it. We'd end up like Shapely. Anyway, the widow and her son are worth siding. I wouldn't run out on them if I had a chance of getting past the Apaches. What did these two do with my guns?"

"They took them into the house, along with mine."

Shannon left the stable, taking the shotgun with him. His rage was slow to subside. As he strode through the darkness of the yard he thought what an opportunity this would have been for the Apaches if Delgado had known enough to apply a constant pressure on a place he wanted to take. It was no thanks to Mathison and Harper that the station still stood. A dim light burned in the house, and the two women stood at the open door. They moved aside as he approached. He entered and stared hard eyed at Belle Larsen.

"You, woman," he slapped the words at her, "don't you ever meddle in my affairs again."

She struck a defiant attitude. "Henry said it was our only hope."

"And your only hope got that drummer killed."

"We don't know he was killed," she said. "The Apaches may not have hit him. Anyway, he was willing to run the risk."

He gazed at her with the rage that was still roiling in him, thinking that maybe some women did deserve an occasional beating and that, if they did, Belle Larsen was certainly one of them. She stood there with dyed hair, painted face, and heaving bosom and felt no guilt over having been a party to sending Ed Shapely to his death. She was cut from the same cloth as Henry Mathison.

Turning from her in disgust, he saw that his rifle and revolver, as well as Murdock's, lay on the table that held the lantern. He picked up and holstered the revolver, then reached for the Winchester.

Looking at Helen Edwards, he felt even more dispirited because of her stricken expression. She at least would be taking it hard that Shapely had been killed.

He said, "The boy is still sleeping?"

She nodded, glancing toward the bedroom. "And Benjy too. Children are fortunate in that they sleep so soundly. Is it possible that Mr. Shapely did get away?"

"It's possible but not likely."

"The poor man . . . but he at least doesn't have to face the terror that is still to come."

Shannon decided it was useless to deny that they still faced the worst part of their ordeal. She was too intelligent to be deceived by false hopes. At the moment he couldn't convince himself that they would survive the Apaches' next attack.

With Murdock gone, Shannon wouldn't have even a slim chance of hurting Delgado and his warriors enough to make them turn back. He went outside and saw the hulking figure of Ben Murdock standing by the well. The man seemed lost in thought, and Shannon supposed he was trying to decide how to get past the Apaches.

He'll make it. . . . Somehow he'll get away.

He thought this with something like resentment.

He started across the yard to take up a sentry post at the wall but was brought to a stop by a scream of terror piercing the quiet night from a distance. The cry was shrill and drawn out, then the silence returned.

Helen Edwards said, "Will, what was that?" Her voice was a hoarse, fear-charged whisper.

"The Apaches," he said, in half-truth. "They're trying to scare us . . . break our nerve. Get inside and shut the door."

She obeyed, and an instant later another terrible scream rang out. The Apaches hadn't killed Ed Shapely. They had taken him alive, and now they were torturing him.

CHAPTER THIRTEEN

Hank Dolan stood beside his stagecoach, a scrawny figure in the darkness. His right arm was in a sling. At Shannon's approach, he spat tobacco juice and said, "A hard way to die, that. The poor bastard should have listened to reason. Me, I'm glad I had no part in sending him out there for them to grab."

Another scream sounded, and Shannon's blood ran cold. He swore under his breath.

Dolan added, querulous of voice, "I oughtn't to have paid any attention to those orders to keep off the road. I'd have made it safe through to Tucson."

"You didn't know Delgado was on his way here," Shannon told him. "For all you knew, he could have been north along the road . . . for you to run into."

"I'd have had a chance of outrunning them," Dolan said. "Holed up here, a man's got no chance at all."

"You don't know that."

"I sure do know it, and so do you, bucko. We're goners, the lot of us. Me, I've about lived out my life . . . and a hard one it's been. But those women and that youngster . . ." He spat again, copiously. "Too bad for them."

The screaming continued at intervals for perhaps half an hour, each agonized outcry diminishing in strength. Finally they ended after a horrible choking sound. Shannon found himself waiting tensely for the screams to resume. But the silence stretched on for some minutes and he relaxed. Ed Shapely's suffering was at an end.

Murdock came to stand with Dolan and Shannon. He was armed now with his revolver and his buffalo gun. "Too bad about that city man." His voice held compassion. "He died hard."

Shannon said, "You're leaving now, are you?"

"I've a mind to."

"What's keeping you, then?"

"Maybe the widow and her kid."

"They're nothing to you, black man."

"They're nothing to you, either, ofay," Murdock said. "Maybe you've got a feeling for the lady, but she's not for you. She's not your kind."

"You're not telling me anything I don't know," Shannon said. "Look. If you're going, go. Don't expect me to beg you to stay."

Grinning, Murdock said, "I'll go in my own good time, white man. And maybe I won't be going at all. Maybe I'll take pity on you and side you when Delgado hits this place again. You're no good alone, you know."

With heavy sarcasm, Shannon said, "Don't keep doing me favors. Anyway, I'm not alone. I have three good men to back me up."

"Old Hank here may be a good man but what kind of shooting can he do with his right arm crippled? As for the other two, they're not worth a plugged peso. That Harper . . . I keep wondering why the Apaches didn't lift his hair a long time ago."

"They were saving him for a time like this," Dolan said. "For when he had a whole crowd here with him, to make it worth their while . . . he not being worth much, himself."

Henry Mathison and Mel Harper came from the stable and made their way to the house.

Watching them, Shannon said, "When the Apaches show themselves, I'm getting that pair out here to lend a hand, if I have to drag them out."

"I'll help you do the dragging," Murdock said. "You keep watch for a couple of hours, ofay. I'm going to get some sleep. I'll spell you later."

He opened the door of the stagecoach and climbed inside.

Shannon said, "Hank, you'd better sleep, too." He moved to the section of wall facing the south end of the gulch.

As he kept watch in the darkness, he found himself thinking of Helen Edwards. Never before had he been so strongly attracted to a woman. The truth was, he wanted her . . . desired her. But Murdock was right: she wasn't his kind. She was accustomed to better than life on a cattle ranch in the middle of nowhere, for even a mining town remote from civilization had more to offer. He chided himself as a poor fool for having let himself be so deeply stirred by her.

To think of her was pleasant, however, and he whiled away the lonely hours with thoughts of her, of her sharing his life. He had become a dreamer because of her, and a dreamer was, he suspected, a person who yearned for what lay beyond his reach.

Relieved by Murdock in the small hours, he slept at his post. He sat on the ground with his back to the wall and cat-napped. He was wakened shortly before dawn by the black man's laying a hand on his shoulder.

"Time to rise and shine, ofay. Delgado and his bucks must be astir by now. If they don't hit us at first light, I'll eat my hat."

Getting to his feet, Shannon said, "No need to say 'if.' They'll come."

He peered south through the gulch, but the hour before dawn always seemed the darkest of the night. For all he could tell, the Apaches could already have returned and taken up positions close to the station. He knew they hadn't, because Murdock, with his cat's eyes, would have spotted them.

"We'll have to keep an eye on the north end this time," he said, "and on the top of the opposite wall as well."

"We'll be busier than a couple of shorthorn bulls put to upgrading a herd of Texas longhorns."

"I'll rouse old Hank and those two sleeping beauties in the house."

"Get the women to rustle up a meal, too," Murdock said. "My belly's gnawing on my backbone."

Shannon went first to the stagecoach, where he woke Hank Dolan and told him to stand watch at the wall facing the north end of the gulch.

As the old-timer climbed stiffly from the coach, Shannon said, "I'll send Mathison to side you with the shotgun. If any Apaches show up there, do the best you can shooting left-handed. There can't be more than a few in that direction. Delgado has most of his band to the south. If Mathison and you can't hold them off, give a yell. Murdock or I will come running."

"If the two of you don't have your hands full," Dolan said.

"Yeah . . . if," Shannon said. He turned toward the house.

Helen Edwards opened the door and looked at him anxiously.

"No signs of them yet," he told her, "but I want to get Mathison and Harper out to the wall. Haven't you slept?"

She shook her head. "I couldn't. I'm too tense."

She started to move aside so he could enter, but he took hold of her arm. She looked at him wonderingly, not trying to pull away. The lantern still burned inside, and in its faint light he could see the soft sheen of her blond hair and the lustrous brown depths of her eyes. Deep shadows lay beneath her lovely eyes, and in the darkness her pallor seemed total. He kept his hold on her arm and drew her closer to himself.

"Not that it really matters, but I want you to know this," he said, "I've never been on the wrong side of the law in my life. Can you believe that?"

"Yes, I can," she replied. "I realize that there is something strange about your relationship with the deputy. It's something other than that of lawman and prisoner, isn't it?"

He nodded. "A private feud. I wore that badge at the start, and he got it away from me when I hurt my leg back in the mountains. He could have left me to die, but he brought me here, and to protect himself posed as a lawman."

"You owe him your life, then?"

"Yes, I owe him my life. But if the two of us get away from here alive I'll do my best to see him brought to trial and hanged." He paused, studying her face. Then, with more feeling than he'd ever before permitted himself, he added, "Somehow it was important to me that you know I'm not the one headed for prison or the gallows. There's one thing more, Helen: that black man and I will do our best to keep you and your boy safe."

"Was it because of Tommy and me that you and he didn't try to save yourselves?"

He smiled faintly. "What other reason could we have had?"

"I'm grateful to you both. I must tell him so, too."

"Tell him when you feed him," Shannon said. "He's worked up an appetite, he says. So have I, to tell the truth. Get the Larsen woman to help you fix a meal for everybody."

She nodded, and he held her close for a moment longer. He looked at her as though etching her features upon his memory for all time. He wanted very much to take her into his arms, but he knew that she, being so recently widowed, would have resented his taking such a liberty. He removed his hand from her arm and entered the house.

Belle Larsen sat at the table, her elbows propped upon it and her face in her hands. She was a picture of dejection, but then, looking at him, she let her expression turn spiteful to show her dislike of him. She had become somewhat bedraggled of appearance. Her red-tinted hair was now untidy. Her powder and paint were worn thin in some spots and had become smeared in others. Her elegant green dress was badly rumpled. He sensed that her floozy's self-reliance was undermined by fear.

He looked beyond her to Henry Mathison, who dozed in a cowhide chair by the fireplace.

There was one who could sleep, Shannon thought sourly. Wrapped in his self-importance, the mine owner probably couldn't imagine that anything could go wrong for him even in such a situation as this. Shannon crossed the room and prodded him with his rifle, causing him to wake with a start.

After staring blearily at Shannon for a moment, he was his usual curt self. "What do you want?"

"I want you outside," Shannon told him. "You're to get a box of shells from Harper, pick up that shotgun outside, and stand guard with Hank Dolan at the north wall. Now move."

Mathison got from the chair, scowling angrily. He'd removed his hat and suit coat, unbuttoned his fancy vest, and loosened his tie and shirt collar. His gray hair had lost its pomaded neatness, his moustache its trimness, his ruddy cheeks their clean-shaven look. The strain of yesterday and the night now about gone had also left him haggard of face.

"You're giving the orders now, are you?"

"That's right. I am, with Murdock's backing."

"The pair of you need a lesson in showing proper respect," Mathison said. "When I get out of this hellhole, I'll see that both of you get it. I'll have his badge and you jailed."

"For now, outside with you," Shannon said. He went to the kitchen.

Finding Mel Harper asleep on one of the table

benches, Shannon prodded him awake with his rifle. The agent had been working on a second jug of whiskey he'd had stashed away. He woke grumbling, pushed himself to a sitting position, and ran his fingers through his matted beard. His bulbous nose was a fiery red. He was far from sober. He gazed at Shannon belligerently.

"What ails you, anyway? Can't you let a man get his rest?"

"You've had your rest. Delgado is due anytime now, and you're to be a member of the welcoming committee. Get your rifle and some shells for that shotgun."

"If I've got to do any fighting, I'll do it from a window right here in this house."

"Any fighting you do then will be too late," Shannon said. "The Apaches will be inside the wall by that time. You'll be out there with the rest of us, trying to keep them from getting into the yard. Your job will be to keep them from shooting down at us from the rim of that cliff yonder. Now get out there . . . move!"

Shannon prodded him again, this time not lightly, and Harper, though still grumbling, did move.

Minutes later they were at their posts, five strong. Calling them that was stretching it a point, Shannon reflected. If they had been five strong in the real meaning of the term, they might have had a fair chance of surviving the coming attack. As matters stood, he felt that Murdock and he could depend only on each other; and being one of two against a dozen or more Apache warriors wasn't the sort of odds he liked.

The first faint light of false dawn crept into the gulch. Soon the nearest rocks and desert growth could be seen, then the long slope leading down into the narrow passage from the south. No movement was to be seen, however, and Shannon looked wonderingly at Murdock. The black man met his gaze with the same uncertainty.

He said, under his breath, "I can't believe it. It just ain't like Apaches to give up without making one good try."

Shannon looked from Murdock's scarred ebony face with its puzzled expression to the north portion of the station wall. Hank Dolan and Henry Mathison were at their posts, peering out through the gulch and evidently seeing nothing to alarm them. He shifted his gaze to Mel Harper over by the well. Sober or not, the agent seemed to be keeping a close watch on the cliff. Over at the house smoke rose from the kitchen chimney, showing that Helen had started a fire on which to cook breakfast. Shannon began to think they might get to eat that meal in peace. And yet . . . he shook his head.

"It doesn't feel right. It can't be that they've cleared out."

Murdock nodded his agreement. “It’s too good to be true.”

Minutes passed, with the early gray light filtering into the depths of the gulch. The Apaches would be easy targets if they came now. This wasn’t like the wily Delgado, Shannon reflected. It wasn’t like any Apache.

A small voice called out excitedly, “Golly wallopers, Mr. Shannon! Ain’t you going to shoot that Injun?”

Looking over his shoulder, Shannon saw little Tommy Edwards running across the yard toward Murdock and him.

“You are going to shoot him, ain’t you, huh?”

Shannon stared at the impish freckled face and realized that the boy was entirely serious.

Caught up by alarm, he said, “What Indian, son? Have you seen one?”

“Sure, I did. That one . . . up there!”

Tommy pointed at the cliff rim, and Shannon saw a warrior standing statuelike there, gazing down at the station. A big man for an Apache; like Ben Murdock, a giant of a man. He was naked except for breechclout, moccasins, cartridge-studded bandolier, and headband. And, yes, a rope about his neck. A rope fashioned into a hangman’s noose. A rifle in his right hand. Delgado, Shannon thought. Delgado calmly sizing up the station and those trapped there.

Shannon shouted, "Tommy, get back into the house!"

He raised his rifle and lined its sights on the motionless copper-hued figure eighty feet above him.

Murdock got off a shot, the report of the buffalo gun thunderous in the narrow confines of the gulch. He missed his mark, and Delgado slowly, seemingly with contempt for those below him, turned and vanished from their sight. He'd taken with him, Shannon was sure, all he needed to know in order to launch another attack on the station.

CHAPTER FOURTEEN

Angered, Shannon said, "An easy shot for a Sharps, and you missed him by a mile."

Murdock shrugged his broad shoulders. "I told you he's got a voodoo charm that works against me." He shoved another fifty-caliber cartridge into the buffalo gun. "What about you, ofay? You didn't even try to bring him down."

Shannon's anger was in part directed at himself. He had no excuse for his failure to get off a shot at the Apache. It was directed at Mel Harper too, since the agent had been told to watch the cliff and yet hadn't spotted Delgado. But for the boy, Shannon told himself, one of them here might now be dead. Delgado had carried a rifle. He would surely have gotten around to using it, given more time.

Shannon looked for Tommy and saw him being hustled back to the house by his mother. He strode in their direction, calling out to Helen.

"Don't punish him," he said. "We wouldn't have known the Apache was there but for the boy."

She gave him a look out of frightened eyes, then nodded that she had heard. As she and Tommy went inside, Shannon crossed to where Mel Harper stood by the well.

"Damn it, man; if Delgado had had a chance

to open fire, it might have been you he aimed at. From now on keep your eyes open."

Harper's bearded face took on a sullen look. "All right, all right. I just didn't see him soon enough."

Shannon swore under his breath and turned from him. This was about what he had expected from the agent. He went to the north side of the yard, where Hank Dolan and Henry Mathison were staring uneasily at the cliff's high rim.

"That was Delgado himself," the stage driver said with an old man's peevishness. "He was an easy shot, and you or that deputy should have nailed him. Ain't that black buck any good at all with his Sharps?"

"That wasn't as easy a shot as you think," Shannon said. "Shooting at a man high above you is always tricky. You two get back to watching out through the gulch and forget about the cliff. I'll be keeping an eye on it from now on."

"Here's hoping you're a better shot than that deputy," Dolan said. "Missing a chance like that. Hell, if he'd downed Delgado, the rest of those red devils would have turned tail and not stopped running till they got back to the reservation."

"Maybe, and maybe not," Shannon said, turning away.

Henry Mathison said, "Hold on, Shannon." He spoke in a flat, demanding tone, still puffed up with self-importance.

Shannon looked at him hard-eyed. "What now?" he said. "If you've just got something sticking in your craw, forget it. This is no time for a fool argument."

Mathison appeared increasingly haggard. His face had lost some of his ruddy color. "Hear me out," he said. "It's my thought that we can dicker with that Apache. According to Hank, Delgado is different from most of those savages . . . a man of some intelligence. Maybe he'll listen to reason, if we get him to parley."

"Look. Don't you know anything at all about the Apaches?"

"I'm not exactly a fool. I've heard tall tales about them ever since I came to Arizona three years ago. All the talk is that it's next to impossible to whip them in a fight. Fighting them is all you people here in the Territory think of. You and the military. Now it stands to reason that if somebody just once tried to come to terms with them, gave them the chance to say what they want—"

"I can tell you what they want," Shannon cut in. "They want to even the score with a few whites for their land and their freedom having been taken from them. Are you going to give that back to them . . . on a silver platter, maybe?"

Mathison swore under his breath. He spoke in a forcedly patient manner. "We could ask for reasonable terms, offer to pay him to withdraw from here."

"Pay them money?"

"Of course. What else?"

"The Apaches have about as much use for money as for a bundle of prayer books. Even if they could be bought, how would we dicker with them? Do you talk their lingo? Do you think they talk ours?"

"What about sign language?"

Shannon shook his head. "There's no easy way out of the fix we're in. This is one time when your money will do you no good at all."

Benjy came from the house as Shannon went to watch the cliff from the middle of the yard. The youth gave him a shy, bucktoothed smile. His china blue eyes were as friendly and trusting as the eyes of a puppy.

"Howdy, Mr. Shannon. What for is everybody standing around with guns like that?"

"Have you forgotten about the Apaches, Benjy?"

"Apaches?" Bewilderment came to the youth's pleasant but dull face. "Reckon I did forget about them. I don't see any. You sure they're close by?"

"They're not far off. And when they come closer, they'll come shooting. You'd better go back to the house so you don't get shot."

Benjy shook his head. "I can't do that. I've got to water and grain the horses. That's my job. Didn't Mr. Harper tell you?"

"Well, get it done in a hurry," Shannon said. "Then go back to the house."

"Yes, sir. I'll do that."

He went on to the stable, not hurrying.

Full daylight had come, but here in the gulch nothing was to be seen of the sun as yet. It would have to climb high before its glare touched the west cliff and crept down to the floor of the passage. Again Shannon thought what a poor location this was for a stage station; it would have been an unlikely site even if there had been no Apaches. Men needed to live where the sunlight touched them.

Helen called to him from the house. "Miss Larsen and I have breakfast ready, Will."

Her use of his given name meant nothing at all except to him, but he was pleased that she did speak it.

"We'll eat out here," he told her. "Harper will come after it." He looked at the station agent. "Get Murdock's first."

"Why him first?" Harper asked, bristling. "What's so special about that black deputy?"

"Just do as I tell you," Shannon said, putting some iron into his voice. "Get his grub, then take some to Dolan and Mathison. You can eat next, and after that you can bring something for me. Get moving."

They did get to eat that meal in peace, though it was an uneasy peace. When Harper finally brought him a plate of bacon and flapjacks and a cup of coffee, Shannon remained standing and continued to watch the cliff rim as he ate. The others had been as vigilant while eating. The threatening though unseen presence of the Apaches could not be ignored even momentarily. They lived with it. The atmosphere seemed charged with it.

Murdock came to Shannon as the latter finished his meal. He was puffing on a Mexican cigar, and he offered Shannon one. As he accepted it and a light as well, Shannon suddenly realized that a strong bond had come to exist between this black man and himself. He felt closer to Ben Murdock than he ever had to another man, despite the fact that they were still enemies. If they survived the Apaches' attack, he would again try to take him to Valido to be hanged. But they were bound to one another, not as friends but as *compadres*, which was, in the Mexican sense, something more than mere comrades. A strange thing, perhaps, but to Shannon's mind understandable.

Murdock said, "If it's Delgado's game to make us edgy, he's sure got me that way. I'd rather have that bunch come and get it over with."

"When they come," Shannon said, "you'll be wishing they hadn't."

Murdock's scarred face twisted with a wry smile. "That could be. You don't suppose, do you, that he decided when he was up yonder that we're too hard a nut for him to crack?"

"You know better than to think such a fool thing."

"Yeah," Murdock said. "I reckon I do."

Delgado kept them waiting throughout the morning, and all of them became edgy. Then at midday the waiting was over, and their edginess became full-fledged anxiety. The Apache chieftain appeared with sixteen warriors. They reined in their ponies at the top of the long grade and gazed down at the station. Drenched by sunlight, their nearly naked bodies gleamed like copper.

"A few more than yesterday," Shannon said as he joined Murdock. "Now we know why our friend waited so long to drop in on us. He had reinforcements coming. There'll be hell to pay if he hits us from the north end and from above as well as from out there. Try beading him with your Sharps. It'll reach that far, easy."

"Ain't no use," the black man said. "Like I keep telling you, my old buffalo gun won't work against his voodoo."

"That's just fool superstition. Let me have a try with it."

Shannon put his Winchester down and took the Sharps from Murdock's hand. The buffalo gun with its long, octagonal barrel was heavy and cumbersome. Shannon rested his left elbow on the adobe wall and drew bead on the bulky figure of Delgado.

"How does it shoot?"

"A trifle to the left," Murdock said. "Not much. Don't allow for it being far off."

Shannon made allowance for the rifle's slight drift, then he squeezed off his shot. The Sharps's heavy report rang in his ears; its kick was powerful against his shoulder. He saw Delgado drop from his pony, but the Apache chieftain had not been hit. Shouting and brandishing his rifle, he sought cover. Except for two, the warriors also dismounted and scattered among the brush and rocks. The still-mounted pair drove the riderless ponies away.

Taking his Sharps back, Murdock said, "Now maybe you'll believe he's got a powerful charm working for him. No use trying to do that devil in. We've got to bring down as many of the others as we can. That's our only hope."

Shannon picked up his Winchester and waited for a target. None appeared. The Apaches had blended with the terrain. None exposed himself to fire at the station. Delgado was still playing a waiting game.

CHAPTER FIFTEEN

An hour passed and a good part of another, and still the Apaches had fired not a single shot. When they finally made their play, Shannon was forewarned. Constantly dividing his attention between the grade and the cliff, he at last saw a movement on the latter.

"Brace yourself," he told Murdock. Then he called out to the others, "You, Harper . . . up there! Dolan . . . Mathison . . . take care!"

Three Indians appeared above, making smaller targets of themselves by lying flat. As they prepared to open fire, Shannon drove a carefully aimed shot at them. The warrior he'd beaded heaved to his feet, staggered one way and another for a brief moment, then lost his balance and plunged over the edge. As that one plummeted downward, Shannon fired at another. Harper's rifle also opened up. A second warrior collapsed, his head and arms dangling loosely while his rifle fell to the bottom of the gulch. The third drew back out of sight.

Murdock's heavy rifle thundered once and then again, and Shannon, breasting the adobe wall, saw two warriors sprawled on the grade. The others there charged downward, shooting as they came. Shannon began firing at the darting, scurrying figures as fast as he could work his Winchester's lever and trigger. He saw another Apache go down and remain motionless. Then he had no more targets. Nor did Murdock. Midway down the slope the Indians had again sought cover. Several shots came from the rocks and brush, then all the rifles out there fell silent as Shannon and Murdock raked the area with a probing fire.

At the far side of the yard Dolan's revolver and Mathison's shotgun took up the fight, responding to several rifles that fired heavily for a brief interval. Shannon crossed to their portion of the wall at a limping run. By the time he reached the pair, no Indians were to be seen north through the gulch.

"How many are there?" he asked.

"Four," Hank Dolan said. "They didn't come close enough for a six-shooter and a scatter-gun to reach them, but we gave them a good scare. They're in those rocks to the right side of the road. I'd rather they wouldn't be. They'll pick us off, sure, if we don't keep down."

"I'll give *them* reason to keep down," Shannon said. He began pumping slugs into the cluster of boulders.

No answering shots came from there. No shots came from anywhere. The Apaches were back to playing a waiting game.

Shannon said, "Mathison, you come with me.

Leave your shotgun." He left his rifle there, propped against the wall.

Mathison followed him without uttering any objection. But he walked draggingly, like a man at the point of exhaustion. His broad face was so haggard it seemed to have aged a dozen years. Shannon led him into the stable, where he took a sack of grain from the pile and placed it on the mine owner's shoulder. Mathison swayed under its weight but then steadied. Shannon took a sack on his own shoulder.

They carried these two sacks and half a dozen others outside and placed them on the north wall to form a barricade. Space was left between the sacks to serve as loopholes. This gave Mathison and Dolan better protection against the rifles of the Apaches concealed among the rocks.

"If they come at you," Shannon told the two, "let them get close enough for your handgun and shotgun to do some damage."

Harper called to him as he started back across the yard. The agent was crouched behind the well wall, gazing fixedly at the cliff top. His bearded face wore a puzzled expression.

"That one we didn't nail . . . he's up to something. I can see him now and then, but never long enough to line my sights on him."

Shannon saw at once that the remaining warrior up there was also building a barricade. He had already pushed some rocks to the cliff's edge.

At the moment he was adding another, without exposing himself. He was on his belly.

"Your eyesight's not too good," Shannon told the agent, and he explained what the Apache was up to. "He'll have to rise above those rocks to fire down on us. You nail him when he does. But, damn it, you'll have to watch close."

"I'll plug him," Harper said with a boozer's false certainty. "Leave him to me."

Shannon rejoined Murdock and asked, "Nothing stirring out there?"

"Not a thing. But I have a feeling that every mother's son in the bunch is looking down his rifle barrel at me. Some of those sacks of grain would do for us. You keep watch, and I'll fetch a few. I can tote two at a time."

He made half a dozen trips to the stable, and with the sacks of grain he brought Shannon built a barricade atop this portion of the wall. It was six sacks long and two high, with narrow openings between each two sacks. Murdock and he could now keep watch without exposing much of themselves to the hidden Apache rifles.

"They're doing mighty little shooting, for Indians," Shannon said. "It's their nature to waste ammunition when they've got plenty."

"You figure they're running low?"

"Either that or they've got no stomach for a fight. But if Delgado was short on nerve, he wouldn't be here at all."

"So they're short of cartridges," Murdock said, "but not so short that they have to give us up as a bad job. I don't see that we have reason to jump for joy just because they haven't ammunition to throw away."

"You're right," Shannon said. "We've nothing to celebrate. Delgado will tighten his siege lines after a while, and he won't have his braves fire on us unless we make easy targets of ourselves. He'll move closer little by little until he's able to launch an attack that will bring the whole bunch right up to this wall and over it."

"That's a happy thought," Murdock said with a miserly grin. "Knowing you is a real pleasure, ofay. I've been having nothing but a good time since I first laid eyes on you."

"That," Shannon replied, "is exactly how I feel about you, black man."

The sun had reached its zenith, and now, for a brief period, the narrow passage was filled with its brassy glare. No air moved down here, and the trapped heat became stifling, suffocating. It felled Henry Mathison, and Shannon, called to the north side of the yard by Hank Dolan, found the mine owner unconscious on the ground.

"He just up and passed out," the old stage driver said. "He's big and full of loud talk, but there ain't nothing to him. You'd better get him out of the sun."

Shannon called Mel Harper over, and they

carried the stricken man to the house. They laid him on one of the bunks in the bedroom, and Belle Larsen, having followed them from the main room, stared at him with dismay.

"My God, he's not dead, is he? Not Henry Mathison!"

Shannon looked at her uncertainly, not knowing if she were upset or merely awed that so important a man had fallen when lesser men endured. He told her that, no, Mathison wasn't dead.

"He's down with heatstroke. Get a wet cloth and wipe him down with it. Give him some water to drink, with a little of Harper's rotgut in it. Not much at a time. After he's come around, get some salt into him."

Helen was at the bedroom doorway, her face pale and taut with strain. He looked at her intently, worried.

"Are you all right?"

"Yes, of course. Don't worry about me."

They moved into the main room, and he had a glimpse of Tommy and Benjy through the doorway to the kitchen. They might have been of an age, for both talked and laughed like small boys. Neither in his innocence felt threatened by the danger outside.

Shannon went to the front door. He turned as Harper, coming from the bedroom, started for the kitchen. Pierced by Shannon's flinty gaze, the agent stopped and gave him a beggar's sorrowful look.

"Just one nip," he said, whining of tone. "My God, it's more than a man can stand!"

"All right," Shannon said. "One short pull at that jug."

He looked at Helen again, letting his gaze linger on her. Her expression changed in a most surprising way. A smile tugged at the corners of her mouth and her brown eyes seemed to light with sudden pleasure.

"It helps me to bear up, Will, my knowing that you care."

"Do I show my feelings so clearly?"

"I'm afraid you do," she said, and came to lay her hands on his shoulders. "In a situation like this, when all hope is gone, a person may as well be honest. So I will be. I've felt during the past three months that I had no reason except Tommy to go on living. Now, when I have only a little while longer to live, I find that I have a second reason. I realize it's too soon for me in my widowhood to say such a thing, but . . . well, it's said."

He now looked at her in a marveling way. He raised a hand to her chin, tilted her face up, and bent to her. Her lips stirred beneath his own in a quick and seeking response, and for the space of a few pounding heartbeats they were alone in a safe world of their own. A rifle shot shattered the illusion as well as the silence, and he turned from her to hurry outside, retrieve his rifle, and face the grim reality that was Delgado and his warriors.

Murdock had fired the shot. He explained that one of the Apaches had started working his way down toward the gulch.

"He ran like a jack rabbit, and I missed him," he said ruefully. "Before I could reload, another of them ran down the slope. More will be trying it, you can be sure."

A moment later a warrior darted from behind one rock to drop behind another. Both Shannon and Murdock fired at him, and missed. As they drove their shots in his direction, a second brave scurried away from a brush clump and flung himself into a hollow place. Both of these warriors were now farther down the grade.

An occasional flurry of shots was fired from out there, covering fire for more of Delgado's braves to move closer to the gulch. The four at the north end of the gulch laid down a sniping fire at intervals, while the one on the cliff traded shots with Mel Harper.

A pattern was now discernible: brief flurries of fire from three directions to cover the advance of Delgado and his braves down into the gulch. The Apache chieftain was closing a trap on the station without cost to himself. By sundown, with dusk gathering in the depths of the gulch, all of the Indians to the south were down from the grade and behind cover. It was clear to Shannon and his companions that Delgado was preparing for an attack during the night . . . that he intended to ignore the Apaches' superstitious dread of fighting in the dark.

Thinking aloud rather than speaking to Murdock, Shannon said, "They'll run right over us. We won't be able to drop enough of them to stop them."

"No doubt about it," Murdock said. "Nothing we can do, though, but fight and die where we stand. It's too late for running."

Struck by a sudden thought, Shannon said, "Maybe it's not. If Delgado holds off until full dark, we'll have a chance of making a run for it. We'll have to take it."

"Ofay, you've gone loco," Murdock said.

Shannon paid no attention to that. He was calling out to Hank Dolan, telling him to come across the yard.

When the stage driver arrived, having come at an old man's stiff-legged run, Shannon said, "Can you handle a team one handed?"

"Sure. Just give me the chance."

"You've got it. Tell Harper to get the harness on the best horses in his bunch and to get them hitched up to the coach."

"We're making a run for it, eh?"

"A run is right. You'll have to head out at a

gallop, to get past those four at the south end of the gulch."

"The whole bunch will come racing after us."

"Forget about that," Shannon said. "Just be ready to pull out in ten minutes or so."

As Dolan turned away, running again and calling out to Harper, Murdock said, "We're not going to make it, ofay . . . and you know it. Once Delgado hears horses being moved about here, he'll know what we're up to. And that's when he'll come swarming down on us."

Shannon had to admit that was not just a possibility but a certainty. "Somebody will have to give him reason not to come swarming," he said. "And that somebody will have to be me."

"Just how are you going to do it?"

"By creating a diversion, as a military man would call it," Shannon said. "When the stage-coach is ready to roll, I'll go out there and shoot up that bunch."

Murdock stared at him in the fading light. "Well, you've elected yourself, ofay," he said. "When I'm safe away from here, I'll remember you now and then . . . as a fool hero."

Shannon didn't reply to that. He set out for the house to tell the people there to prepare to make a run for it.

CHAPTER SIXTEEN

His nerves taut, a queasy feeling in his stomach, Shannon watched with a growing impatience as Mel Harper and Benjy hitched up the six-horse team to the stagecoach.

He tried to will them to get the job done. *Hurry it up, for God's sake! Get a move on!*

So far, everything had gone smoothly. He was afraid that something would go wrong at the last moment. He took a worried look beyond the adobe wall, half expecting to see Delgado and his warriors launching their attack. He couldn't quite credit it that the Apaches hadn't caught on to what was being done here in the station yard.

The stagecoach had been rolled back from the gateway in the wall and turned about so it faced the opening. Harper and the dull-witted youth had brought the horses from the stable in pairs, backing each pair into the traces and getting it hitched. They hadn't wasted any time, really, but to Shannon it seemed they were taking forever.

Hank Dolan was ready to climb to the driver's seat. Henry Mathison and Belle Larsen were already inside the coach. Shannon had helped the woman support the ailing man during the walk from house to rig. Mathison still wasn't himself, but he had the shotgun with him and was seated on the right side so he could, if necessary, fire at the Apaches in the rocks to the north of the station.

Seeing nothing of the Apaches out there in the darkness, Shannon turned to Helen Edwards and her son.

He picked Tommy up and said, "So long, son. You be a good boy and mind your ma."

He handed the boy inside to Belle Larson, then took Helen by the arm. He was touched by a deep sadness at this moment but managed to smile for her.

"Listen: if you don't want to go back East, there's a place for you at Valido," he said. "Go there from Tucson and look up Henry Yates at Amhurst's general store. Tell him I said that you're to live in the Amhursts' house and help him run the store. Tell him that I want you paid the same wages he gets."

Helen looked bewildered.

"I own the store and the house," he told her. "I came into them when the Amhursts, my sister and brother-in-law, died. If you do go there and if I shouldn't show up, the store is to be yours and Yates's in partnership and the house wholly yours."

Now Helen appeared alarmed. "You're not coming with us?"

"I'll be along later," he said. "Now get aboard."

She tried to hold back, but he forced her to get into the coach.

He turned away at once, crossing to where Murdock still stood guard at the south wall. He picked up his rifle.

"They're doing a lot of stirring around out there," Murdock said. "They must be catching on that something funny is going on here."

"Better get yourself aboard that rig. Hank might go without you."

"No chance of my letting him do that."

Shannon said, "I've only one regret, black man. You can probably guess what that is."

"I can guess. It bothers you because you didn't get to see me hanged."

"That's it. Now clear out, damn you."

"I'm going," Murdock said. "No use my wishing you luck. It would do no good. So long, ofay."

He strode toward the stagecoach.

Shannon ran along the wall to the rear of the yard and there eased himself over it. Keeping close to the base of the gulch's west cliff, he moved away from the station for about a hundred feet, making his way past rocks and through brush. He raised his rifle and fired the shot that was the signal he had arranged with Hank Dolan.

He heard the old-timer's voice lift in an unholy yell, heard too the pistol-shot crack of his whip. Then came the sound of the horses and stagecoach in motion. The Apaches began an excited yelling. He saw them now as they broke from cover and ran after the rig. Alarm knifed through him, for they were closer to the station than he had believed. They might be able to bring down Dolan's horses!

Rifles cracked. Muzzle flashes stabbed the darkness. He began firing at the running, shadowy shapes. He saw one and then a second fall. He saw too that five or six turned in his direction. Their wild shooting told him they had not actually spotted him. He shouted at them, cursed them, and fired twice more. They came on, wholly intent upon him. But the others, the larger number, pursued the stagecoach, firing heavily. Noise and confusion filled the entire gulch. Now, abruptly, Shannon was too busy fighting for his life to determine whether or not Hank Dolan and his passengers were making it safely away.

He knew the Apaches' numbers now. Five warriors were bent on bringing him down. They rushed toward him, howling their war cries and shooting as though they had plenty of cartridges. He leveled his Winchester over a boulder, took careful aim, and squeezed off his shot. The nearest warrior went down. He targeted and dropped another. The remaining three sought cover and began sniping at him. He fired two more shots, then he left the boulder and moved farther along the base of the cliff. They did not see him go. They continued to shoot at the position he had abandoned. Coming to a brush thicket, he crawled into it and dropped to the ground.

He had gained a respite, though it would be but a brief one. His heart pounded wildly, and his breathing was labored. He told himself that he was not afraid to die. He was in fact fatalistic about death coming to him now, in this place, at the hands of the Apaches. If a fear did lurk deep within him, it was the fear of all mankind through all the ages when the end was at hand. This was not cowardice but an inherent part of the human consciousness; it was a dread of the unknown, of what lay beyond the transition from life. He, Will Shannon, had long ago convinced himself that he had both his beginning and his ending here on earth. And yet how could he be certain of such a thing?

This inborn fear did not make him craven now during the little while left to him. He would stand firm until an Apache bullet found him. Or until he turned his revolver on himself so that he would not be taken alive and tortured. Sadness touched him more heavily than this fear, as he thought of Helen Edwards and of what his life might have been if he could have gotten away with her and the others.

But had they gotten away?

He became aware that rifles were still firing,

from over by the front of the stage station, he thought. He heard the thunderclap report of a weapon of larger caliber than the Indians' Winchesters. He knew it was Ben Murdock's buffalo gun. The knowledge filled him with despair. The stagecoach hadn't made it safely out of the gulch. Hank Dolan must have been shot off the box, his horses killed in their traces. Only the black man was returning the Apaches' fire. Shannon heard no blastlike reports of a shotgun, no revolver shots. It had been for nothing, then. Helen and Tommy, and the others, had not escaped.

For the first time in his adult life Will Shannon tried prayer. *God, please . . . please don't let them be taken alive!*

Murdock's Sharps sent its heavy blast once more into the night. The agonized scream of a hit warrior echoed the report. One more of Delgado's braves had gone down. But there were so many, and Shannon, visualizing them swarming over and killing the black man, rose and left the brush thicket. He had no thought of helping Ben Murdock. He was not thinking at this moment but merely acting on the urge of some primal instinct that was also inherent in man.

CHAPTER SEVENTEEN

Shannon had no sooner left the brush thicket than he saw the three Apaches he'd fired on from the boulder. They were stalking him, two off to his right and one to his left. When he became aware of the latter, that one had his rifle raised and aimed. Now, before Shannon could bring him under fire, he squeezed the trigger of his weapon. The hammer fell on an empty chamber. Instead of the expected report, there was only a sharp click.

The warrior reacted instantly and with as much ferocity as speed. Rushing at Shannon, he swung his rifle like a club. Shannon ducked aside and fired from the hip. The slug caught the Indian in mid-leap, and he dropped in a crumpled heap almost at Shannon's feet.

Shannon swung about to face the two others. Only one of the pair fired at him, and he realized that Delgado's band was indeed short of ammunition. He traded shots with the one who still had cartridges, to no effect. He turned and ran, not as much in flight from them as to reach the fighting that continued hotly farther through the gulch. They came after him, running with great bounding strides while he, handicapped by his still hurting knee, moved at an awkward, sluggish pace.

He came to the station's south wall and put his back to it. His pursuers were so close that he fired pointblank into the one, then was forced to drop his rifle and take the other on with his bare hands. The Apache had thrown away his rifle and was striking at him with a knife.

Shannon pivoted, and the point of the knife merely ripped his shirt. The Apache slammed into him, and the knife drove into the adobe of the wall with his second thrust. Shannon managed to lock his left arm about the warrior's neck, and they went around and around in a macabre sort of dance as they struggled against each other. He felt the Indian's hot breath on his face and had the acrid body odor of the Indian in his nostrils. He drove a punch to the warrior's ribs, then let loose of him and clubbed him in the kidneys.

Grunting under the blows and losing his balance, the Apache fell against the wall. He slumped there, his teeth bared in an animallike snarl and his eyes glinting dully with hatred. He feinted with the knife as Shannon tried to close with him again. Backing off, Shannon stared at him; and the Apache stared back. Time stood still while they took each other's measure.

Dimly, Shannon became aware that there was silence all about them. No rifles racketed, no warriors howled. He and this brave, a tough, wiry little savage, might have been the only ones left alive in the gulch. His adversary too seemed aware of this, Shannon saw. He stilled his labored breathing and tilted his head in a listening attitude.

Shannon had been acting by instinct all the while since he had fired his first shot at the hostiles. Now reason returned to him, and he thought, *Listen, you: there's no sense in our trying to kill each other.*

He stepped back, well back, and spread his empty hands.

"Damn it," he said, all but shouting, "let's call it quits!"

He might as well have saved his breath. The Apache did not understand his words. He would have ignored them if he had understood. He tensed, gathering himself to spring. He held the knife low for an upward thrust at the white man's guts.

Shannon started to reach for his rifle but thought better of it. The Apache would be on him the instant he bent down. He drew his revolver, but, as the warrior lunged at him, instead of thumbing back the rifle's hammer he swung the weapon like a club. Again the knife ripped his shirt, and this time it sliced through flesh as well. But the thrust did not penetrate deeply, for Shannon's blow landed hard to the Apache's face the same instant the blade drove home.

The warrior was again knocked against the wall. He dropped his knife and put his hands to his savaged face. Blood spurted from his nostrils. He appeared dazed to the point of helplessness. After a long moment he began moving along the wall away from Shannon. Suddenly he realized that the white man did not intend to kill him. He started away at a stumbling walk and disappeared into the darkness.

Alone and seemingly safe, Shannon let himself sag against the wall. Reaction had set in, leaving him weak and shaky. His mind reeled, and he could not quite credit the fact that he had survived. He felt no exaltation over having come through it all. Too much blood had been spilled, too many lives lost. He was the victim of a depression that was almost despair. At this instant he did not know that he wanted to be alive. He could not see that he had anything to live for.

He was bleeding slightly from a gash just above his belt, but he had no pain. The wound was superficial. He removed his bandana neck scarf and folded it into a pad. Unbuttoning his shirt, he laid the pad against the cut and rebuttoned his shirt. His spirits remained at low ebb. Physically, he was exhausted. He was about to sink to the ground to rest when a voice, real or fancied, called to him.

"Shannon? You hear me, Shannon?"

Murdock's voice.

Shannon shook himself mentally, thinking his imagination was playing tricks on him.

"Murdock? You there, Murdock?"

"I'm here, all right, ofay . . . what's left of me."

"Where?"

"In the yard, over by the well."

Now Shannon was certain, and he experienced a rise in spirits over knowing he was not alone in the world. He picked up his rifle and with an effort pulled himself onto the wall. He lowered himself down its inner side and then walked slowly, limping, across the yard. Murdock sat on the ground, his back to the wall of the well. Despite the darkness, Shannon saw that the right sleeve of the black man's shirt was wet with blood from shoulder to cuff.

"How bad is it?"

"My arm or the fix we're in?"

"Both."

"I've leaked a lot of blood and I've got some pain. I'm out of cartridges, but the Apaches don't know it. They're out, themselves, anyway. If they weren't, they would have done for me. I've lost my six-shooter. Dropped it when I got hit."

"They're still around, are they?"

"What's left of them. Delgado's gone loco. He won't call it quits. He wants us bad, for messing up his plans. He's out there somewhere, trying to jack up his nerve and make one last try. He don't know I've got a hole in me any more than he knows I'm out of cartridges. How about loaning me your handgun?"

Shannon handed Murdock his revolver, took cartridges from his pocket, and refilled his Winchester's magazine. Murdock shoved the gun into his holster.

"When I heard you yell yonder, I thought I was dreaming," he said. "I figured you were dead. What were you doing, holding a parley with some of them, or have you taken to talking to yourself?"

"I was trying to talk one of them out of using his knife on me."

"I wouldn't put such a fool stunt past you, ofay. How'd you manage to stay alive all this while?"

"Mostly by dumb luck," Shannon said. "Listen: we'll have a better chance if we move into the house. Can you get up . . . walk?"

Murdock struggled to his feet and stood swaying as though assailed by weakness. He laid a hand on the well wall to steady himself. He looked at Shannon with a rueful smile.

"This time, ofay, it'll have to be you helping me."

Shannon took Murdock's left arm over his shoulder and put his own right arm about the man's middle. They began moving slowly toward the house. They were still ten yards from it when a scurrying sound warned them of danger.

Murdock burst out, "Let loose of me!"

Shannon was already pulling away from him. Facing about and bringing his rifle up, he saw five shadowy figures rushing at them through the darkness. The Apaches had come silently, their moccasined feet making only a whisper of sound. They were so close that Shannon fired pointblank into the nearest warrior. As that one went down, he levered another cartridge into the Winchester's chamber. He had no chance to fire again, however, for another brave leaped at him and tried to down him with a blow of his rifle. As he dodged the clubbing weapon, Shannon felt his injured knee give way. He fell to the ground, landing with a jolt. As the Indian lashed out at him again, Shannon heaved over in a frantic roll. The stock of the swung rifle struck the ground only inches from his head. He rolled over again, then rose to one foot and one knee. He fired into his adversary. The slug took the brave between the eyes and knocked him over backward.

As Shannon came erect, throwing another cartridge into the Winchester's chamber, two of the three remaining Indians turned tail and fled. They ran from the yard, disappearing into the darkness. The third was grappling with Ben Murdock, and Shannon, seeing that he was as hulking of figure as the black man, knew him to be Delgado.

Shannon tried for a shot at the Apache chief but found it difficult to bead him. Delgado and Murdock were locked in a deadly struggle. They went around and around, fighting silently but savagely. The black man had his revolver in his hand but was unable to get its muzzle set against the Indian's body. He held it in his right hand, and his wound was in his right arm. Delgado was armed with a knife, but Murdock had a grip on the wrist of the hand that held it. Suddenly they fell to the ground, rolling this way and that as each strained for an advantage.

Shannon saw a chance for a shot. He fired and missed. The two combatants were in such a tangle that he dared not shoot again for fear of hitting Murdock. The black man tried using his gun as a club, but there was no strength in his arm. He let the gun drop and grasped the rope that the Apache wore about his neck as a symbol of his hatred for all men who were not of Apache blood. Now Murdock took a fearful chance. At the risk of the knife's being driven into him, he let go of Delgado's wrist and placed his left hand too on the rope. With his two-handed grip on the portion of the rope tied in a hangman's knot, he heaved to his feet. He moved around behind the Indian, barely avoiding a thrust of the blade. Somehow he found the strength to haul Delgado erect and then jerk him off balance.

Despite the darkness Shannon saw their faces clearly. Delgado's was contorted with fury and the beginning of apprehension. Murdock's was stiff with strain and, no doubt, with pain as well. They stared at each other, their teeth bared in snarling grins. The Apache's knife hand moved slightly to and fro like the head of a sidewinder about to strike. When he made his move, Murdock gave a violent pull on the rope and hurled him against the side of the well. Delgado would have toppled over the wall and plunged downward but for the black man's hold on the hangman's noose.

Shannon had a clear bead on Delgado now. He shouted at Murdock, "Don't move! I've got him!"

"Keep out of it," the black man said. "I'm going to finish him . . . on my own!"

Delgado remained slumped against the wall for a moment, then he hurled himself at Murdock with the knife striking at Murdock's throat. Murdock again jerked him off balance and hurled him away. This time he let go of the rope. Delgado landed asprawl ten feet away. Before the Apache could pick himself up, Murdock dropped down on him. The black man had drawn his own knife, and now, as they thrashed wildly about on the ground, he drove it into Delgado's throat. Blood gushed, and Murdock threw himself away from it. He fell onto his back and lay so still, except for his raspy breathing, that Shannon, staring at them both with a sense of horror, feared that the black man too was dying.

CHAPTER EIGHTEEN

Shannon half carried, half dragged the unconscious Ben Murdock to the station house. He got him inside and somehow found the strength to lift him onto one of the bunks in the bedroom. He lit a lantern, feeling it now safe to show a light.

He used his pocketknife to cut away the bloody right sleeve of Murdock's shirt to get at the wound. The bullet had gone through the shoulder and had certainly shattered bone. How the man had been able to fight Delgado to the death, Shannon couldn't imagine. He found cloth and applied a heavy bandage, hoping to stem the flow of blood. Murdock had bled more than he could afford; his black face had taken on a grayish tinge and his lips were a purplish hue.

The bandaging done, Shannon covered him with a blanket and went to the kitchen. He poured whiskey from Mel Harper's jug into a tin cup and added some water to it. Returning to the bedroom with the cup, he found that Murdock had regained his senses and was looking at him with glassy eyes. He raised the man's woolly head by slipping his left arm beneath it and then held the cup to his mouth.

"Whiskey and water," he said. "Get it down."

Murdock drank it greedily. "I could do with

more, ofay." His once deep, rich voice was now a weak croak. "A lot more. I'm famished."

Shannon went for more of the watered whiskey, and Murdock drank it no less greedily. He gazed at Shannon wonderingly.

"Why so downcast?" he asked. "You ought to be jumping for joy, now that you've got me and can take me in for hanging. Ain't nothing I can do now to keep you from it."

"I'll be taking you in, but that's nothing to celebrate," Shannon said. "How's a man to feel good about anything after what's happened and all the others are dead?"

"What are you talking about, ofay?"

"The people on the stagecoach."

"Them? They ain't dead. They got clean away."

Shannon stared at him disbelievingly. "But you . . . ? I thought you were the only one who escaped from the stage."

"I wasn't ever on it," Murdock said. "I figured it couldn't get past those Apaches at the north end of the gulch. So I went out there and did some shooting. I kept them so busy they didn't get off more than a few shots at the rig."

Shannon thought, *Helen's safe . . . and Tommy too.* That the others—Hank Dolan, Mel Harper, Benjy, Henry Mathison, Belle Larsen—were also safe didn't much matter to him. He was glad for them, but for him only Helen and Tommy Edwards counted. He had been so completely convinced that the stagecoach had not gotten away that the news of its having escaped was a shock to him.

He said, "I could do with a drink," and went to the kitchen to tap Harper's jug again, this time for himself.

Shortly after dawn, just after he had fed Murdock some hot broth made from boiling jerky in water, Shannon stood at the door and watched a company-sized detachment of cavalry come into the gulch from the south and pull up in front of the station. The column consisted of about forty officers and troopers, several pack mules, a civilian scout, and half a dozen Indian policemen.

The Indians, somewhat ludicrous in their blue uniforms, got down from their ponies and went scurrying about like so many hound dogs sniffing out a scent. The officer in command dismounted his men and then rode into the yard with the civilian scout. After the latter had swung over to the well and looked at the Apaches lying dead there, he rejoined the officer.

"One of them's Delgado, Cap'n," he said, something like awe in his voice. "And, so help me, whoever done him in did it with a knife."

The pair came on to the house, reined in, and looked at Shannon in a wondering way.

About forty years of age, lean of body and bronzed of skin, the captain had the sharp-honed look of an officer who had spent his entire career on one frontier or another. The scout was a whiskery, leathery man shabbily clothed in a mixture of white man's garb and Indian buckskin.

The officer said, "Captain Vorhees, sir, at your service." He smiled sardonically. "Now don't say the obvious: that the military is always rendering its services too late." He nodded in the scout's direction. "Tom Briggs."

"Better late than never, gentlemen," Shannon said. "I'm glad to see you, believe me. My name is Shannon . . . Will Shannon."

"You're the only survivor?" Vorhees asked.

"There's another man. He's laid up with a bad wound."

Briggs was unable to hold his curiosity in check. "Who used the knife on Delgado? You?"

"Not likely," Shannon said. "It was the man inside, Ben Murdock, who fought it out with him. And he did for the Apache after he himself had been shot and was bleeding like a stuck pig. It was quite a go-around."

"That it must have been," Briggs said. "I would have bet a month's pay that no man alive could get the best of Delgado hand to hand. This Murdock must be *mucho* hombre. I'd sure like to shake his hand."

"He's plenty man, all right," Shannon said. "But maybe you won't want to shake his hand when you see him."

"Why not?"

"He happens to be black."

"Hell, I'd shake his hand if he was a Chinaman," Briggs said, dismounting. "Coming along to see this black-skinned wonder, Cap'n?"

Vorhees nodded. He twisted in his saddle and called out to one of his lieutenants, "Mr. Jenkins, you will form a burial detail and have it police this entire area. A common grave, of course. Pick a site at the end of the gulch."

Shannon said, "There's a dead white man somewhere at the north end. He'll be in bad shape. The Apaches took him alive. I'll be obliged if your men bury him in a grave of his own and build a cairn over it as a marker. His family may want to claim the body when they're notified. We should see if there's anything on his person telling where he's from: an address, maybe."

"You didn't know him?"

"Only that his name was Ed Shapely and that he was a city man, a drummer."

"How did he happen to be here?"

"He was one of the passengers on the stage that was caught here when the Apaches showed up."

"He was the only person killed?"

Shannon nodded. "We got the others off last night, when it seemed as though the hostiles would come over the wall."

Vorhees looked at him with mounting interest. "Let me get this straight. The stagecoach pulled out while Delgado was hitting the station?"

"That's right, Captain."

"And it got past the Apaches?"

"It did, but it took some doing," Shannon said. "We managed to save the stage driver, four passengers, the station agent, and his helper."

"I took you to be the agent."

"No, I'm not that. I just happened to come along at the right time, with Murdock. Or maybe it was the wrong time. Anyway, the two of us stayed behind to give the stagecoach a covering fire when it pulled out."

Vorhees shook his head as though finding this difficult to believe. Dismounting, he said, "Mr. Shannon, yours is a story I want to hear in detail. From you and Murdock, if you don't mind."

Shannon took him and the scout inside to meet Ben Murdock, and he introduced the black man to them with something like pride.

The cavalrymen moved out to track down the remnants of Delgado's band, once the slain Apaches and Ed Shapely were buried. Shannon occupied himself with caring for Ben Murdock, cooking meals for them both, and looking after the horses in the corral. He still had much empty time on his hands and found idleness far from his liking. He kept wishing the stagecoach would start running again. He was impatient to leave the station, and of course he knew the reason: he wanted to get to Valido and see if Helen and her son had gone there. She had not said that was her plan, but she had committed herself to him, so he believed, by saying that his interest in her had given her a second reason for living. She had spoken those words under stress, however, and she might since have regretted them and gone East.

Damn it, she can't have! She's my woman!

He told himself that but was not convinced it was so.

The stagecoach returned late in the afternoon of the third day. Hank Dolan had only Mel Harper and Benjy for passengers. He was not making the run to Lode City this trip, he explained.

"I've orders to take you and Murdock to Tucson," he told Shannon, "if that's where you're headed." Then he added, "Word reached there from the Army that you and the black man were still alive. It came just last night. It was mighty good news, because nobody figured that you and Murdock had any chance at all."

"You got through that night without any trouble, did you?" Shannon asked. He was eager for word of Helen and Tommy.

"The hell we did," the old man said. "We just made it by the skin of our teeth. Look at them bullet holes. I tell you, them Injuns almost did for the lot of us. Ain't that so, Mel . . . Benjy?"

The dull-witted Benjy nodded in agreement, but Harper, saying, "It sure is," winked broadly to let Shannon know that Dolan was exaggerating.

Then, his bearded face turning sober, the agent said, "We did lose Henry Mathison, though. He got plugged trying to use the shotgun. If he'd kept down, he wouldn't have been hit. He was still alive when we got to Tucson, but he cashed in his chips a couple of hours later."

"Too bad," Shannon said, but he felt untouched by the mine owner's death. "What about the other passengers?"

"None got even a scratch," Mel Harper said.

Shannon drew a relieved breath. Helen was all right, and so was the boy. He wanted to ask if the two had taken the stage to Valido or the train East. He didn't, however. He was afraid the answer would be the one he didn't want to hear.

"When will you heading back?" he asked Hank Dolan.

"Yeah, when are you?" Ben Murdock said.

He came across the yard with an invalid's dragging step. He carried his wounded arm in a sling that Shannon had rigged for him. But his wound was beginning to heal and his strength was returning. He looked almost his normal self.

With a half-grin on his scarred face, he said, "Not that I'm eager to be on my way. Shannon's taking me to Valido to hang. You've noticed that he's wearing the star now, haven't you?"

Shannon had taken back the deputy's badge and pinned it to his own shirt front.

Dolan shook his head. "After all you two have

been through together it somehow don't seem right."

"It's right," Shannon said, "and he knows it."

"It's right," Murdock said, "because I'm crippled and unarmed, and he ain't. Like the old saying has it, might makes right."

They got underway at dusk, after Hank Dolan had eaten supper, with a fresh team in harness. Shannon occupied one seat, the backward-facing one, and Murdock the other. The trip would take all night, and the black man, in anticipation, lay on his left side and folded his big frame into the small space he occupied. He seemed to sleep. Shannon wasn't sure that he did.

Shannon felt that Murdock was too docile and resigned. He now knew him as well as he knew himself, and he believed the man was hatching some scheme to avoid being taken to Valido. Fearing him even though he had no gun and but one serviceable arm, Shannon spent all those hours of travel keeping watch on him. This gave him time to ponder the strangeness of their relationship. He still blamed Murdock for Kate's death; he always would hold Murdock responsible for it. But he had come to respect and even admire him as a human being. He realized that he would find no satisfaction in seeing him hanged. And yet . . .

He's got to hang. No matter what, I can't let him off.

They rolled into Tucson at dawn, pulling up at the stage depot. The town was only beginning to wake.

When they got from the coach, Murdock said, “Only a short trip to Valido now, eh, ofay?”

Shannon was carrying his saddlebags, his own rifle, and his prisoner’s buffalo gun. He heard himself say, “I’m not taking you there, black man.”

Murdock’s ebony face broke into a grin that twisted his ugly scar and showed his gold tooth. “I didn’t figure you were. When did you get around to knowing it?”

Shannon’s gaunted face was all sour angles. He wasn’t at all pleased with this sudden reversal of his decision. He felt that he was failing his dead sister. And the law as well.

“I didn’t know until just now,” he said. “And I don’t know what changed my mind, unless it’s the kind of man I know you to be.” Angry with himself, he took it out on Murdock. “Damn you, black man, why did you have to kill her—a man like you?”

“To my mind, your sister’s getting killed was an accident, because I didn’t want it to happen. But you won’t see it that way, even if I argue with you till we’re both blue in the face.”

“You’re right,” Shannon said. “I won’t ever see it that way.”

He propped the buffalo gun against the rear

wheel of the stagecoach, then turned to enter the depot to find out when he could make connections for Valido.

"You, there, Will . . ."

Shannon faced about with a scowl. "Get out of my sight. I don't want anything more to do with you."

"I've a present for you. Catch . . ."

Murdock tossed a small object he'd been holding in his left hand.

As Shannon caught it, the black man said, "If you keep on wearing that badge, you'd better search the next hombre you arrest." He picked up his Sharps, said, "So long, friend," and strode down the street.

Shannon looked at the object he held. It was a double-barreled derringer pistol, a weapon much too small to fill a man's hand and yet big enough to kill with.

He had this all the while . . . could have killed me anytime.

For a moment Shannon was shaken, then he realized such a thing would never have happened. Murdock would not have been taken to Valido to be hanged, but he would have avoided it by some means short of killing him. Suddenly Shannon knew, as he should have known all along, the black man's weak spot, if it could be called that.

He can no more kill if there's another way out than I can.

He'd killed Phil Amhurst, but for what he considered good reason. He'd killed the Apaches only because he'd been forced to, and then reluctantly. He could have killed him, Will Shannon, time and time again. No, there was nothing of the killer in Ben Murdock.

A rueful grin curled Shannon's lips. Murdock had given the derringer to him for a reason: *To let me know he figures he's the better man . . . and it could be he's right.*

Shannon turned into the depot, pocketing the sneak gun. He would keep it as a remembrance . . .

A stage made the Valido run three times a week, and today—a Saturday, Shannon learned—was one of those times. He had a few hours before the rig pulled out to buy himself a change of clothing and take it to the barber shop, where he had a bath in the backroom tub and then, in his new duds, let the barber give him a shave and a haircut. He was left with enough time to get breakfast.

Since there were but two other passengers, he had a seat to himself. He settled himself as comfortably as possible to try to catch up on his sleep.

While growing drowsy, he told himself, *She'll be there. Valido was a better offer than back East.*

A voice in his mind mocked him, *You're loco.*

A woman like that . . . she's a lady and you're about as much of a gentleman as a long-horned bull running wild in the brush.

She would be at Valido or she wouldn't, and if she weren't he would be one disappointed hombre.

He slept on it.

Ordinarily the trip took eight hours. Today, midway, the stage ran into sluicing rain and the going was slow for the last twenty miles. It pulled into Valido more than two hours late. Except for the saloons the business places, which stayed open until nine o'clock Saturday nights, were already closed. The townspeople would be turning in. Even so, Shannon told himself, he wasn't waiting until morning to find out if Helen was here.

As he got from the coach, he wondered what he would tell Sheriff Milt Owens when he turned in his badge. The truth, of course. The old lawman was a reasonable sort and would understand why he had let Ben Murdock go.

But the sheriff could wait. Shannon strode through the rain, which was now only a light drizzle, to the side street where Phil and Kate Amhurst had lived. Upon seeing lamplight through the curtained windows of the house, he felt like letting loose with the now almost forgotten Johnny Reb yell.

He knocked on the door and after a moment

Helen's voice reached him with a cautious, "Who is it?"

"Will Shannon, Helen."

She unlocked and opened the door. She was prepared for bed, wearing a robe with a flower design over a nightgown and bedroom slippers. Her blond hair hung at her shoulders in two thick, gleaming braids. Her smile revealed her pleasure in his coming.

"Come in, Will," she said. Then, laughing, she added, "That is absurd, my inviting you into your own house, isn't it?"

"Your house," he said.

He removed his hat, placed it and his rifle and saddlebags on a chair, then looked at her without trying to hide the depths of his feeling for her. She was made uncomfortable by his appraisal. A flush heightened the color in her cheeks.

Womanlike, she said, "I look a mess. If I'd known you were coming tonight . . ."

"You knew I'd come through it at the stage station?"

She nodded. "I didn't leave Tucson until word came that you were safe."

"Do you like it here?"

"Very much. Of course, it's only been two days . . ."

"And Tommy?"

"He loves it. He's always made so many friends."

"He's in bed?"

"Yes, he is. If you'd like to see him . . ."

He shook his head. "Let him sleep. I'll see him in the morning. I just stopped by to make sure you had come. I'll go over to the hotel, and . . ."

He made no move to leave, finding that he couldn't take his eyes off her. She was lovelier, more desirable, than he had remembered. He moved to her and took hold of her hands. Her lustrous brown eyes grew round, startled.

"Will, not so soon. It's been only three months, and—"

"It's been a lifetime for me," he said. "But if you have doubts about my being right for you . . ."

"Oh, no . . . not that," she said. "My heart and my mind tell me that this is what I want, after a proper length of time."

Suddenly he cared nothing at all about propriety. She would have to accept him as he was, even to his faults—if impatience was a fault. He drew her into his arms. She held back briefly, then with a little cry of surrender gave herself wholly to his embrace.

As he bent to her lips, he told himself, *I owe this to Ben Murdock. But for him I would never have met her.* Then the thought was gone, and he gave himself up, mind and body, to the promise of this woman he had found when his only future seemed a bullet from an Apache rifle.

Center Point Large Print
600 Brooks Road / PO Box 1
Thorndike, ME 04986-0001 USA

(207) 568-3717

US & Canada:
1 800 929-9108
www.centerpointlargeprint.com